ST. AUGUSTINE ACADEMY PRESS

About *Rev. Henry S. Spalding, S.J.*:

Henry Stanislaus Spalding was born in January 1865, the fifth of eleven children of William and Isabel Spalding of Bardstown, Kentucky—six of whom eventually entered the religious life. The Spaldings themselves came from a long line of devout Catholics who were among the early settlers of the Colony of Maryland, and could count among their family relations not one, but two bishops: The Most Reverend Martin John Spalding, Archbishop of Baltimore and The Most Reverend John Lancaster Spalding, first Bishop of Peoria.

As a Jesuit priest, Spalding taught at Creighton, Marquette and Loyola Universities, helped establish the Medical schools of the last two, and wrote or edited seven books on ethics and sociology. However, he is best known for his adventure stories, which captured the imagination of a generation of readers.

About *The Cave by the Beech Fork:*

The Beech Fork River passes by Spalding's hometown of Bardstown on its way toward the Ohio. This area is rich with history, being the first Catholic Diocese west of the Appalachian Mountains, settled shortly after the Revolutionary War, as well as being a center of whiskey production from early times. Even Daniel Boone spent time in Bardstown.

The Cave by the Beech Fork is a story set in the Bardstown area around the time Spalding's grandfather was a boy, and includes actual historical figures such as Father William Byrne and Bishop Flaget. At the end, we are told that this story, as well as its sequel, *The Sheriff of the Beech Fork*, was found in an attic of the main character's family home...so how much is fact and how much is fiction? No one today can say...

HE DREW HIS REVOLVERS AND STEPPED QUICKLY TOWARD THE TWO MEN.

THE CAVE BY THE BEECH FORK

A STORY OF KENTUCKY
~1815~

By Rev. Henry S. Spalding, S.J.

2015

ST. AUGUSTINE ACADEMY PRESS

HOMER GLEN, ILLINOIS

This book is newly typeset based on the third edition
published in 1901 by Benziger Brothers.

The original text has been modified slightly in places
in order to smooth awkward parts in the dialogue;
this was done only where necessary, and with great care and
respect for the era in which it was written.
The name of one of the characters was also changed,
due to a consistency error in the original story.

This book was originally published in 1901
by Benziger Brothers.

This edition ©2015 by St. Augustine Academy Press.
All editing by Lisa Bergman.

ISBN: 978-1-936639-46-5
Library of Congress Control Number: 2015950183

Contents

A Note to Readers

THIS BOOK was written in 1901 and depicts life in the Kentucky wilderness in 1815. As such, it contains negro characters—freed slaves—using a form of language common to the people of that era. Terms we now consider unacceptable were used. We attempted to replace terms now considered offensive, but to rewrite all the dialogue would have come off sounding awkward and out of character. Therefore, we have left all but these few terms just as the author wrote them, because they accurately portray the language and character of the times they depict.

On the other hand, we did modify other portions of the dialogue in order to make it flow more freely as would be common among boys, opting to replace "let us" and "it is", etc. with "let's" and "it's". These contractions were widely used throughout the book already, so we felt this to be entirely appropriate as well as helpful to the modern reader.

Lastly, an inconsistency in the names of characters was discovered toward the end of the book: the runaway slave had been identified as Mose, whereas Mose was actually the freeman living with the Howards who had *helped* the runaway slave. Therefore we have changed the runaway slave's name to avoid confusion.

In Christ,
Lisa Bergman
St. Augustine Academy Press
Feast of the Transfiguration, 2015

The Cave by the Beech Fork

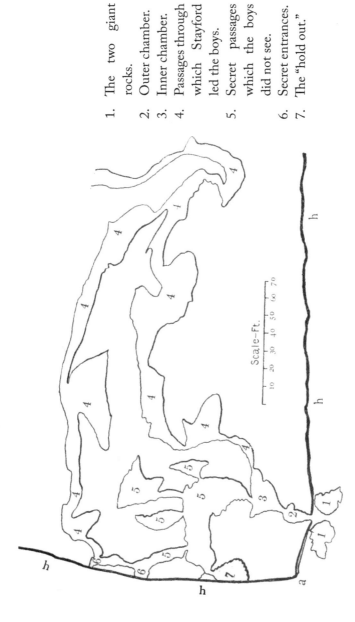

1. The two giant rocks.
2. Outer chamber.
3. Inner chamber.
4. Passages through which Stayford led the boys.
5. Secret passages which the boys did not see.
6. Secret entrances.
7. The "hold out."

Scale–Ft.
10 20 30 40 50 60 70

Ground plan of Cave—The heavy line marked *b, b*, represents the hill running along the Beech Fork, turning abruptly at *a* and following a small creek.

CHAPTER I.

A Day's Hunt
Along the Beech Fork.

"**N**O WONDER this river is called the Beech Fork," said Owen, as he rested his trusty rifle by his side and pointed toward the thickly-clustered beech-trees, which skirted the banks of a small stream.

"See, too, how close they are to the water's edge; they have taken the place of the sycamore and willow," said his companion, Martin Cooper, at the same time seating himself upon the trunk of a fallen tree and looking in the direction indicated.

"But do you notice anything peculiar about those beech-trees?" asked Owen.

"Yes; they have long, slender branches."

"And the leaves—see how green they are, while the others are beginning to fade."

Beautiful, indeed, was the scene before them! The myriad leaves of the underbrush and the lofty canopies of the trees were dyed with all the varied colors of an autumn day. Even the thistle, when sheltered by some impending bough, retained its rose-pink bloom. Patches of sumac nestling close to the ledge of rocks, where larger growth could not survive for want of moisture, raised their cones of crimson berries; the sour-gum was laden with clusters of purple fruit as tempting to the eye as the most delicious grapes; the hickories were conspicuous by their russet foliage; the deep-lobed leaves of the white-oak were burning with fiery red; the ash-trees, scattered here and there, were robed in garments of purest saffron: only the beech-trees remained unchanged by the autumn frosts, for their small, serrate leaves were as green and glossy as during the summer months. Beech, beech, beech; who could number them?

Here nature seemed to have prepared for them a paradise. Other trees grew there only to bring out by contrast the boundless, unbroken forest of beech-trees.

"The old forest is a fine place during this month," said Martin. "Still, I prefer not to spend the night here. Let us start home, it's getting late."

"I'd like to have at least one shot at a turkey before we go," replied Owen. "Say, Frisk," he continued, addressing a bird-dog which was enjoying a good rest at the side of his master, "old fellow, can't you find a turkey for us? Why don't you work as Bounce does? Hear how he is barking and chasing that rabbit."

He had scarcely uttered these words when both boys were startled by a sudden noise. The leaves rustled, the underbrush of the woods separated and a large deer bounded past them. Each sprang for his rifle but it was too late; before either could fire, the coveted prize disappeared behind a ledge of rocks.

As they stood there, rifle in hand, they were, in dress at least, perfect types of western huntsmen, though neither had seen his sixteenth year. Owen Howard's entire outfit was in harmony with the wild and rugged scenes around him. His gray trousers made of coarse home-spun cloth, his deer-skin hunting jacket, his fox-skin cap and sturdy moccasins, all bespoke a life far removed from the busy scenes and worldly comforts of town or city. He had a bright, piercing eye, a countenance frank and winning, a voice as clear and musical as the call of the meadow-lark. He was as nimble as a squirrel. There was about his whole person an air of singular freedom, and every part of his well-shaped frame was perfectly developed by continued though not overtasking labor.

The friend who stood beside him was dressed in the same unique hunter's costume. He appeared less active, but more robust than his companion. His face was ruddy, round, and freckled; his long, unkempt hair fell in reddish clusters from beneath his hunting cap. A look of thoughtful earnestness was stamped upon his features as he stood and gazed at the place where the deer had disappeared.

"Probably it'll cross Rapier's Ford," said Owen, recovering from his surprise. "It's been a favorite crossing for them of late. There's no harm in trying. I would walk a week for a shot at that fellow."

"All right. Let's hurry on fast," said Martin.

So the two pushed on at a brisk rate toward the ford about a mile below. They posted themselves so as to cover the narrow path which approached the river, and waited in true huntsman-like silence. An hour passed, and no sound of the faithful dog could be heard. At last, far over the hills his bark was faintly audible. Then the alarm became louder, and a slight click of their rifles showed that the boys were preparing to give the deer a warm welcome. If it was far ahead of the hound, as usually happened, it might rush by them at any moment. Suddenly their attention was drawn to a spot by the rustling of leaves, and peering from behind the trees they saw a large turkey-gobbler, strutting along wholly unconscious of the danger near at hand. What a fine mark it made as it strolled deliberately by with its head erect and wings arched! Owen was the first to see it and raised his rifle to fire; but as Martin signed to him to wait he lowered his rifle and let the turkey pass by. Judging from the barking of the dog, the deer was making for the ford. Owen felt comforted for the loss of the turkey, for if the deer passed between them one or the other would certainly bring it down.

"How I would like to wring the neck off that turkey!" muttered Martin to himself, for the gobbler persisted in remaining within rifle-shot, scratching among the dry leaves, and making as much noise as a whole flock of turkeys.

The boys were disappointed in their expectations, for the deer changed its course, and again left the river. Another hour passed, and the deep shades of the forest cast a gloom on all around.

"Helloo, there, Owen!" shouted Martin, emerging from his place of concealment, and stretching his cramped limbs. No answer came, so he called again in a still louder voice: "Helloo, there, Owen! Wake up, and let us move; it's getting dark."

Still no answer came.

"Owen! Owen!" he called, walking toward the place where his companion had waited. Not finding him, Martin took the horn which hung at his side and was about to raise it to his mouth, when he heard the report of Owen's rifle. The latter had given up all hope of killing the deer, and had crept cautiously away in quest of the gobbler. He had just caught sight of it in the thick underbrush, but the woods were now so dark that his aim was not true.

"We're in a pretty plight," said Owen as Martin approached. "Hunting all day, and nothing to show for our work but a few squirrels."

"Yes!" assented Martin. "And it's seven miles home—dark, too; in half an hour we won't be able to see ten steps ahead. We stayed at the ford too long; there's no going home to-night, and that is all about it. Why, an Indian would get lost a night like this. We must stay here; it won't be the first night we've slept on the banks of the Beech Fork."

"That's all right for the summer," argued Owen. "But remember that it's October now, and the nights are frosty."

"What's to be done?" asked Martin, glancing anxiously around the dark forest.

"I really don't know. But I do know one thing: I'm tired and hungry."

"Let's stay here. We won't starve. We'll have the squirrels for supper."

"Then we'll stay. Squirrels for supper, a soft bed of leaves, and a fire to drive away the frost. What else does a fellow want?"

"I'll bring Bounce to the camp," said Martin, blowing a loud blast on his horn.

A deep bark answered the echoes, and soon the faithful dog stood panting at the side of the young huntsmen.

"Why didn't you bring the deer this way, old fellow?" asked Owen.

Bounce shook his head, as if to say that he did his best, but could not succeed.

"Well, come on. You've worked hard, and shall have a good supper," said Martin, as the two boys set to work to prepare for the evening meal.

A large pile of wood was collected, and a fire was started against the trunk of a beech, which stretched its thick branches on all sides, forming a natural tent. Martin constructed two cups with the leaves of a paw-paw-tree, and filled them with clear water from a brook near at hand. Owen had the squirrels dressed in a jiffy. One was suspended over the fire by a green twig, while the other was wrapped in damp paper and placed under the live coals to roast. Thus, two different dishes were prepared from the same meat. They had also some dry bread left from their luncheon. Uninviting as their repast may seem to some, to them it was more savory than the most tempting viands, having, as it did, the true Spartan seasoning. Bounce and Frisk were not forgotten. They shared in the day's spoil, and gnawed at the bones until far into the night.

Owen and Martin now collected a large heap of leaves before the fire, and placed their rifles near by in readiness to receive any wildcat which chanced to be attracted by the light.

Their last and most important duty was that which every Christian performs before retiring to rest. Our young friends had pious parents; they had lived in an atmosphere of simple but deep faith, and would have considered it almost a crime to neglect their morning or evening prayers. There, then, they prayed; at night, and in the stillness of a forest, where giant trees stretched out their branches like the arches of some great cathedral, and where all around was hushed in holy silence.

"I do believe it's going to rain," said Martin, catching a glimpse of the clouds through a rift in the trees as he lay down upon his rustic bed.

"Why didn't I think of it before? I—I don't see how I forgot it—I intended to tell you about it—and it is not a mile away," muttered Owen in a half audible tone.

"What are you saying? Are you dreaming?" asked Martin.

"I was talking about a cave which I found last month when chasing a 'coon—a big one, too."

"What, the 'coon?"

"No! the cave. If it rains to-night I'll take you there. It's better than a log-house."

"Perhaps it's the one that Mr. Rapier told me about the other day," said Martin. "It's in this neighborhood, but no one knows the exact spot. Long ago, even before Daniel Boone came to Kentucky, the Indians used to live in it during the hunting season."

"Are there two large rocks before it?" inquired Owen, raising himself up to a sitting posture and staring at Martin with evident interest.

"Let me see; I believe he said something about two rocks. Now I recollect; there were two large rocks, one on each side."

"That's the place; and if the rain doesn't drive us there to-night, we'll see it to-morrow morning."

Owen then lay down again, and was soon fast asleep, dreaming that he discovered an immense cave, whose entrance was guarded by two dogs as large as the two rocks which he had seen. His dream was scarcely more wonderful than the wonders which that cave really contained.

CHAPTER II.

Owen And Martin Visit the Cave.

IT WAS far into the night when the boys awoke. The fire had burned low, and the rain which had been falling for an hour began to penetrate their leafy canopy.

"Owen! Owen!" cried Martin, the first to awake, "it's raining."

Owen was stiff from the chilly night air. He rubbed his eyes and stretched his limbs for some minutes before he realized his situation.

"Wake up! wake up!" Martin remonstrated, at the same time throwing a handful of damp leaves into the sleeper's face as an additional inducement. "You had better take me to that wonderful cave," continued he.

"I dreamt about the place," said Owen, who was now fully awake, "and that the two rocks had been turned into dogs."

"You must have been enjoying your dream, for I thought you would never wake up. I was just going to put a little fire into your moccasins," replied Martin.

"That would have brought me in quick time, for a fellow can't sleep and be roasted at the same time. But come, let's start. It's pretty dark, and I'll have to turn Indian to find the cave a night like this."

"Keep your weather-eye open, Bounce," said Martin, turning toward the dog. "Our rifles are damp. If there is a wildcat in the neighborhood, you must do the fighting. Do you hear, old fellow?"

Bounce shook his head as if to say there was no danger while in his company.

After plodding along and elbowing their way through the damp bushes, the boys reached a hill which ran along the bank of the river for many miles, rising at times to the height of some three hundred feet. Carefully they clambered up toward the two giant rocks which could scarcely be discerned in the gloom, Bounce occasionally giving a low growl of alarm as they approached.

Again and again they stopped and listened, but nothing could be seen or heard. They therefore concluded that it was only a fresh trail, and that the animal itself was not near.

"I tell you it's dark," said Martin, who was the first to pass between the two immense rocks into the cavern.

"Dark as a dungeon," replied Owen in a tone of voice that showed he was not exactly pleased with the situation.

"All we need is a little fire to make things look home-like," said Martin, at the same time searching for some dry wood.

As no wood could be found the boys were forced to remain in the dark cave. Crouched together in a dry corner they tried to sleep, but could not. Bounce continued to growl, and, since he never gave a false alarm, they did not feel perfectly at ease. A strange and subdued sound seemed to issue from the crevices of the rocks. Both boys listened, yet neither spoke. Was it the dripping of the water from the damp arches above? What could it be?

"Didn't you hear something?" asked Martin.

"I thought so," replied Owen, "but, when I listened again, I heard nothing except the dripping water."

Here their conversation was interrupted by a low growl from Bounce.

"Something's wrong," said Martin. "I can't sleep here without a fire. Let us look for wood again."

As they groped around in the dark searching for wood, Martin slipped, and at the same time grasped the side of the cave to prevent his falling. The huge rock yielded, and opened like the massive door of some great dungeon, disclosing a lurid light farther in the cave.

"Heavens! what is this?" gasped the boy, losing his hold and letting the rock swing back to its former position.

"A robbers' den," whispered Owen, trembling with

fright. "They haven't seen us; let's get away as fast as we can."

Fortunately, the dogs did not bark. The boys would have left the place unobserved, had not a man met them at the entrance.

"Who are you?" demanded he, in a gruff voice.

"Two boys; we were overtaken by the night, and had to sleep in the woods. It commenced to rain, and we came here for shelter," said Owen.

"Youngster, don't tell me a lie! Is there no one around here except yourselves?"

"No, sir! No one!"

"How—a—did you come to know about this cave?" asked the man in a milder but hesitating way.

"I found it one day when I was out hunting," answered Owen.

"I found it in the same way," said the man. "The rain drove me in here, too. It isn't a very good place to sleep; still we'll have to hold out here until morning, so just lie down, boys, and try to take a rest."

"No, sir!" said Martin, looking toward the place where the big door had opened. "We are going to leave this cave immediately. It's a robbers' den or it's haunted."

"What! What did you say!" demanded the man, all his former gruffness immediately returning.

"Robber's den! haunted!" stammered Martin, excitedly. "There's a big door to the left. I opened it and saw a light."

"You did? You did? You saw a light in there?" growled the man. "Then, boys, you've seen too much to leave here until I let you go. Don't try to run away, or I'll kill both of you!" and he emphasized his threat with an oath, at the same time swinging open the door and ordering the boys to go into the inner part of the cave.

They obeyed tremblingly, and saw the rock door locked behind them.

"Now, boys," said the man, "this isn't a robbers' den. It isn't haunted, either. If you sit down there and keep perfectly quiet, I won't hurt you. But if you don't do as I tell you, you'll get into trouble." With these words he left them, and passing through another door went farther into the cave.

Our two young hunters were so frightened that neither spoke for some time.

By the flickering light of a fire which had been kindled in the center of the chamber they could examine their dingy prison. It was more than eight feet high and twenty feet long, with solid rock walls and incipient stalactites projecting from above. Skins of minks, foxes, raccoons and wildcats were stretched on forked staves the full length of the cave; and from their variety and number one would infer that he was in the rude home of a trapper. Nothing else was visible, not even a rough bench or a bed of straw. No doubt the occupant of this mysterious cave had other apartments connected with this one.

Martin was the first to break the awful silence.

"What a fool I was," gasped he, "for telling him—about that door."

"Well, it's too late to cry about it now," replied Owen. "Are you much frightened?"

"Why—I was so scared—that I thought—I should never recover—my power of speech."

"My heart stopped beating."

"If mine stopped—it is making up for it now. It isn't beating—it's hammering."

"I must confess that I don't feel very brave just at present," said Owen, trying at the same time to force a laugh.

"I only wish we had Bounce in here with us," replied Martin.

"Yes, I'm never lonesome in the woods when I have him with me. But, say, Mart! did you notice that when the man left us, he opened another door there to the right, and that there was another light farther in the cave?"

"No; are you sure?"

Owen was about to answer, when the door in question was swung aside, and the man entered, wearing a mask and carrying a bright torch.

"Well, boys," said he, "I see you didn't try to run away. I've been thinking the matter over, and have come to the conclusion that I'll let you go. Of course, you'll have to promise not to say anything about the cave."

"We'll promise that," said Owen.

"And you will have to keep the promise."

"Oh, we'll do that, too," replied Martin.

"Glad to see you so willing; but we'll settle the whole matter in the morning. Don't be afraid, I'm not going to hurt you. Lie down and try to rest until I come back. The ground is a little hard, it's true, but it is dry; and there is no danger of catching cold."

He extinguished the few smouldering coals in the middle of the cave, where a fire had previously been kept burning to dry the skins. After again admonishing the boys not to move, he took his torch and departed, leaving them in utter darkness.

CHAPTER III.

In Which Owen and Martin Learn More About the Wonderful Cave.

WALTER STAYFORD was not the sole occupant of that mysterious cave; he had a companion with him by the name of Jerry. The two men lived in a hut, about three miles from the cave, and passed for trappers. They were well known to all the neighbors, and were both musicians, and often supplied the music for rural dances and picnics. Jerry especially was sought for, and it was considered a privilege to have the jolly big fiddler on the music stand. Whenever he was to play, a special mention of the fact was found in all the notices which announced the dance itself. On such occasions his big, round face was one perpetual smile, his fiddle seemed fairly to talk, and so much did he add to the pleasure that he received the appellation of "Jolly Jerry." The two trappers spent weeks and months in the cave and accounted for their protracted absence from their home by pretending that they had gone on long hunting expeditions into the central part of the State. Every spring they went south on one of the many flat-boats or rafts, which carried the products of Kentucky to the ports along the southern parts of the Mississippi. There was a third man, who frequently visited the cave, and who was more directly interested in its secret than either Stayford or Jerry. His two friends generally called him "Tom, the Tinker."

As the night gradually wore away, the three men were seated around a dim fire, warmly discussing the fate of the two boys.

"Shoot 'em! shoot 'em," demanded Tom, the Tinker. "If you two don't do it, I will! They must not leave this cave!"

"Tom, you is drunk or crazy!" said Jerry. "Shoot two boys for a little chink; never! Not for this cave full of gold and whisky!"

"No one can find it out," replied the Tinker. "People will think that they were drowned, that they shot each other, or that something else happened to them."

"I'll do anything but kill," said Stayford; "that I'll never do. I once knew a murderer who was haunted by a ghost day and night. Besides, what good would it do?"

"It'll save this cave and everything in it!" said the Tinker; "besides, those boys are Catholics! I hate them!"

"Tom!" cried Stayford, jumping to his feet, "don't say anything against the Catholics around here, or I'll make you swallow one of these red-hot coals. I'm a Catholic, or I should be one. Yes! I—I am one, and don't you say anything against them!"

Tom was silent.

Stayford looked at him defiantly, and continued, "I told you before, Tom, not to run down the Catholics, and if you do so again you've got to take back your words, or whip Walter Stayford!"

"Darn my buttons!" interposed Jerry. "Here you is fighting again. I'll club both of you until you feel like wild cats under a dead-fall if you keep on fighting. I reckon we'll turn the boys loose, and—"

"Be ruined, robbed, sent to jail!" interrupted Tom.

"If you want to lose every cent you has, Tom, and be hauled off to Louisville and hung, just kill them boys! Just kill them, and you'll have every man in the country on the trail, like so many hounds, and they'll follow us up till we're caught!"

"Yes," chimed in Stayford, "and you'll have these holes full of ghosts."

"And if you'd bury them a thousand miles deep, they'd be found. They'd come up to the top to tell on us somehow, darn if they wouldn't," said Jerry.

"But boys can't keep secrets!" argued Tom.

"I reckon they can, if we do it this here way. Let 'em know that we are on to 'em, and if ever they says one word about this here cave, we'll burn their father's houses, and play thunder in general. I reckon that'll fetch 'em."

"Well, Jerry," said Tom, "it would be pretty hard to kill two boys for such a small thing. I don't like your plans, but you have been as sly as a red fox since we started in the business, and if you haven't lost your senses, I know you will run things all right."

Tom became himself again as soon as he was convinced that his money was safe. His last words on leaving the cave at break of day were: "Run it well, Jerry! run it well!"

"Yes, run it well," repeated Stayford, as the Tinker closed the door and left him alone with Jerry. "We've done all the running. Tom couldn't have done it by himself. You have done the scheming—I helped, and the old miser has made the money; that's the only thing I hate about it."

"And we ain't stored away much," said Jerry.

"No! I am tired of working for the old miser; but I'll stand by you, Jerry. You have always stood by me and helped me, and I'll stand by you."

"I reckon we had better shake on that, Stayford. You is for a fact the bestest friend I ever had. Walter Stayford never went back on nobody."

"I never went back on a friend, Jerry, but I did go back on my Church, and I've been thinking of it ever since I don't know when."

"Don't get chicken-hearted; when you are old and about to kick the bucket, I reckon you can make it all right. You see, foxes don't start to run till they hear the dogs."

"That's the reason the fools are caught—and you want me to do the same with the devil."

"No! Stayford, keep away from him. I never seen him, but they say he's not good company."

Jerry then set to work to prepare breakfast for the boys. He had been his own cook for twenty years, and could get ready a repast on short notice. The breakfast on this occasion consisted of fried rabbit, johnny-cake and rye-coffee.

In the meantime, Stayford took a torch and went in to arouse the boys. He found them sleeping soundly.

"Now, boys," said he, awakening them, "I'm going to set you free. But first I want to show you the size of this cave, and then, while you are eating your breakfast, I'll tell you why I've shown it to you. Did you have a good rest?"

"Yes, sir," replied Owen. "Almost as well as if I was at home."

"We agreed to keep awake," said Martin, "and then it seemed to me that I dozed off and you came in and called us immediately."

"Oh, no!" said Stayford. "It has been over four hours since I left you. I was afraid that you wouldn't be able to sleep, because I frightened you so much by my cursing and so on. You see, boys, I was very mad when you told me that you had seen inside of the cave. But it's all right; so don't get scared any more. Now, I'll show you the size of this place. It would take a whole day to see all of it. I only want to show you a few ways I have of getting in and out."

Leading from the interior of the cave to the chamber where the boys had spent the night there were two passages; one was in the center just opposite to the rock door through which Stayford had introduced his frightened prisoners, and the other to the right of this latter entrance. Through this second opening Stayford passed with the two boys. To let them enter the first passage would reveal the secret he wished to conceal from them.

The part of the cave through which the boys were led appeared a little world in itself. Sometimes they were forced to stoop or crawl along, and then they were suddenly ushered into a spacious apartment, whose size was magnified a hundred-fold in the dim, uncertain light of the smoky torch. How dreamy and ghost-like it seemed! Strange, weird shadows flitted silently along the uneven walls, then suddenly disappeared, as if affrighted by this unwelcome intrusion of beings of flesh and blood.

"Wait a moment and I'll let a little light into the cave," said Stayford, passing before a large flat rock, which he began to remove from its place by means of a lever. Several smaller stones were then thrust aside, and the light of day burst in upon the young prisoners.

"Look!" cried Owen. "The sun is shining."

"Can't we go out this way?" asked Martin, stooping

down and peering out into the bright forest.

"Not unless you wish to break your necks, for the hill outside is perpendicular and fully twenty feet high. Besides, I want to show you another way I have of getting in and out of the cave. Afterward you must look down into the 'bottomless hole'; that's what we call it. It runs right through the world to China."

"There," he continued, after walking but a few feet. "If you fall into that well you'll land in kingdom come."

The boys approached the place cautiously. Before them they saw a round opening about six feet in diameter, which appeared to be the work of man—a dark, cylindrical passage cut through the solid, limestone floor, a portal black and forbidding that led to the abodes of endless night. Yet it was formed by the hand of Nature; when or how no mortal could tell.

"Listen, boys, listen!" Into the hole Stayford threw a large stone.

It rasped against the walls of projecting rocks. It bounded from side to side, while the vaults above moaned with the prolongation of repeated echoes.

"Down!" Stayford paused.

"Down-n-n!" Silence again.

Owen held his breath.

"Down! down-n-n-n!"

Martin grew dizzy and unconsciously grasped the hand of his companion.

"Down! still, still falling," whispered Stayford, as the noise grew fainter and the echoes ceased. From the seemingly immeasurable depths below came sharp, quick notes like the tick of a clock; then silence, stillness—strange, oppressive, deathlike.

In his pocket Stayford had carried several stones of different sizes. These he cast into the hole at intervals, the larger first and then the smaller. The effect was most deceptive. The boys really imagined that they heard the single stone falling many hundred yards below.

But all the wonders of the cave had not yet been seen.

Passing on to another room, which seemed to be the largest which they had yet entered, the guide again paused, and grasped a large grape vine, which hung from the ceiling.

"See this vine," said he; "I'll give it a slight jerk; now watch what happens." He pulled the vine slowly. At the same time a huge oak beam was gradually rolled to one side, leaving an opening five feet high and nearly three feet broad.

"This is my work," continued Stayford; "look at it carefully, boys, and you will see how nicely it is balanced. Three men could not lift this beam, and still I can swing it around with one hand. But I have showed you enough; let us go back to the place where we started. In ten minutes you will be on the road home."

"Why don't you let us out here?" asked Owen.

"Then you would know two ways of getting into the cave; as it is, you will not be able to find this door again."

Stayford pretended to lead the boys by a different way, but in reality he took them over the same ground, passing through one of the apartments three times. This Owen and Martin could not observe, for their torch gave scarcely sufficient light to secure a safe footing.

On reaching the place where they had spent the night, the boys were again ordered by their guide to wait, while he went to bring them the frugal breakfast which had been prepared for them. After they had satisfied their appetites, they followed Stayford out of the cave. Here they found Bounce and Frisk, who wagged their tails and barked with evident joy at the sight of their masters.

Stayford had put on his mask again, so that his features were entirely concealed. "Boys," said he, "you are now free; but before you go, listen to what I say to you. In the first place, I know both of you. This is Owen Howard; this is Martin Cooper. I know where you live; I even know Father Byrne, who goes to Owen's house to say Mass. I am not a robber, I never hurt any one. You see, I found this cave, and want to make some money on it by charging people for going through it. The land around here belongs to old Louis Bowen; and if ever he finds out about the cave, he'll not sell. After I have bought the property, then you can tell everybody in the State, but until that time you must keep it secret. Keep it secret! a dead, dead secret! not a word! not a word about it to any one! If you do—if you do—I'll, I'll hurt you, kill you, burn your father's houses. I am not a bad man, I am not a mean man, but this is the only way I have of making a living, and you must not spoil it on me. I have been half starving myself here for a long time, trapping and working around to make enough money to buy the land. I have shown you how large the cave is, and how many ways I have of getting in and out to let you know that no one can catch me. If old Bowen comes around here I'll know that you told. So remember now; a dead, dead secret until you hear that I have bought the cave. It may be ten years before I can buy it; then I'll let everybody know about it."

Without waiting for an answer, without a parting word, he waved his hand and disappeared in the cave.

Owen and Martin, as soon as they had recovered from their surprise, shouldered their rifles and started homeward.

CHAPTER IV.

The Howards.

AT THE CLOSE of the 18th, and the beginning of the 19th century, many Catholics emigrated from Maryland to Kentucky. One of these was a farmer named Zachary Howard. He sought a home where he and his family could enjoy the comforts of their holy religion, and for this end consulted Father Byrne, the resident pastor of Bardstown. Father Byrne had for some time been in quest of a settler who had means sufficient to buy a farm about nine miles east of Bardstown, and to erect a house which could be used as a stopping place for the priest who attended to the spiritual wants of the neighborhood. Such a one he found in Mr. Howard. The good man was overjoyed at the honor to be conferred upon him. Yes, what an honor! to have the Catholic families assemble beneath his humble roof,

and the holy sacrifice of the Mass offered in his own
dwelling.

As soon as Mr. Howard had occupied his new
home, he set to work to improve it. For miles around,
except a few scattered clearings, there was one
continuous, and in many places impervious forest.
The wooded lands bordering on the Beech Fork river,
about half a mile from the Howards, were as wild and
unbroken as when the Indians fought and hunted in
the "Dark and Bloody Ground." The labor of hewing
down the large oaks and hickories, or of "clearing," as
it was commonly called, was a Herculean one. Mr.
Howard, however, was equal to the task before him.
Although in his fifty-sixth year, he was as strong and
active as a man of thirty. After ten years of hard and
patient labor, he was the owner of a large and well
stocked farm, with more than one hundred acres of
rich land.

Before removing to Kentucky Mr. Howard had
freed his four slaves, but they were so attached to him
that they remained in his service and continued to call
him master. The first among them was "Uncle Pius"
(the old negroes were usually called Aunt or Uncle), a
venerable and superannuated negro with hair as white
as cotton. He was no longer able to endure steady
work in the fields; however, he was useful in many
ways. The wooden hinges, and wooden latches, and
wooden locks; the strong oaken benches, and rustic
chairs, with corn-shuck bottoms; the hominy mortar,

the linsey and carpet loom; the busy and indispensable spinning-wheel, the miniature wind-mills, which shifted and buzzed incessantly on the top of the corn-crib; the martin-box perched high above the meat-house, inviting the winged travelers to stay and rest: all these were made by the deft hand of Uncle Pius. It was he who tended the kitchen-garden, trained the young tendrils along the new arbor, and propped up the young pear-trees, when they were no longer able to support the fruit which they bore.

The noisiest creature around the house, excepting the guinea-hens, was "Aunt Margaret." Her talkativeness seemed to increase with age. In her own opinion, she was the most important factor of the Howard household, and she often wondered what people would do when she was dead. With all her prating, and babbling, and chatting, Aunt Margaret, like Uncle Pius, did what work she could. Hour after hour found her at the loom. She handled the shuttles adroitly; and few, even among the younger generation, could send them flying forwards and backwards as fast as she.

The last negro worthy of mention was one who bore the distinguished name of George Washington Alexander Hamilton Howard. Washington was in his tenth year. He was a typical negro of the old stamp; as black as charcoal, with a flat nose, large mouth, and thick lips. He did not, however, put much value on personal beauty; and, provided the watermelon crop did not fail, he was the happiest of mortals.

He was indebted to a ruse of Aunt Margaret for his historic and sesquipedalian name. At his baptism she insisted on his being called George Alexander. When the sacrament had been administered she clapped her hands with joy and announced the rest of the name. No amount of persuasion could make her change the monstrous appellation or drop a single syllable. Whenever the boy was wanted she had ample time to call out: "Gawge Wasenton Elexander Hamilton Howard! Come heah quick, chile." Owen was the first to dishonor the historic title. Being something of a wag, he gave him the sobriquet of "Wash." All with the exception of Aunt Margaret approved of the amendment, and the great George Washington Alexander Hamilton Howard was addressed by his monosyllabic name.

*   *   *   *   *   *

It was an early hour of the morning to which we referred in the last chapter. Mr. Howard arose and taking a long tin horn, which hung from a peg on the wall, blew it three times as a signal for all to arise. The summons was answered by Uncle Pius, who thrust his head out of the half opened door of the cabin where the negroes lived, and exclaimed: "We'se a gittin' up, massar."

In a few minutes all assembled for morning prayers. These were always said in common, according to the pious custom introduced by the early missionary priests of Kentucky, and still practised in many Catholic families.

When prayers were finished the day's work began. A fire was kindled in the big stove of the kitchen, which was soon savory with fried mutton, bacon, and cornbread. Out in the woodyard one of the negroes was busy with his axe, cutting enough firewood for the rest of the day. No part of the farm presented life so noisy and varied as the immediate vicinity of the corn-crib, where thirty-seven fat and hungry hogs were grunting and clamoring for their breakfast. As soon as Mr. Howard mounted to the top of the crib and opened the door, there was a general scramble to get just beneath it, although he always threw the corn fully twenty feet away so as to scatter the hogs and be able to count them. Up from the pond marched the whole family of ducks, led single file by the old black drake. The geese were not slow in coming for their part of the corn, marching in a solid phalanx, with the little yellow goslings in the center, to protect them against the dog Frisk, who seemed to enjoy charging the whole army and routing it by his own unaided efforts.

Then came the chickens, and the turkeys, and the guinea-hens, and the calves, and the heifers; and there was a most harmonious chorus of voices—the grunting, bleating, gobbling, quacking, lowing; all pleasing sounds to the old farmer, who enjoyed the scene, and scattered the corn profusely.

"Didn't see anything of Owen down the lane?" he inquired of the negro workman who was driving the cows in from the clover field.

"No, massar! didn't see nuthin' of 'im down dar."

"I hope he didn't stay out in the woods all night. I thought that he had stopped with Martin and would be home by this time, for he knows that we need him to help us get the wheat in."

"Kindar col' out sure last night; and hadn't it rained the 'simmons (persimmons) would got some frost on thar eye-brows."

"I shouldn't have let Owen go. But he was so anxious to look for those wild turkeys that I thought it better to give him permission."

"If he stayed out last night he'll have frost in his bones sure," said the negro.

"Well, we shall have to wait and see what has happened," replied the farmer. "But look, Mose," he continued, pointing toward a thin column of smoke rising above the tree tops. "I reckon old Bowen has had another fire. I've been watching that smoke for some time; it is too much for one chimney. The poor old fellow has had his corn-crib burned twice in the last three years. I trust that he has not suffered the loss a third time, for he takes it so hard. I thought he would die of grief the last time his crib was burned."

"It do look jus' like a fire's been burnin' up dar, sure," said Mose.

"I don't understand how his corn-crib is set on fire,

for he never lets the men smoke around it."

"Smoke around de corn-crib," replied Mose, with a prolonged emphasis, "why, bless de Lord, he don't let 'em smoke nowhar. He's de holdenest on ole fellar to his money ebber I seed; he don't let dem niggars get 'nough to eat."

"How would you like to work for him?" inquired Mr. Howard.

"'Drudder die right heah on de spot," said Mose.

The breakfast horn blew and the two walked slowly toward the house. At the yard gate they met Uncle Pius. He was always delighted when consulted about matters of grave importance, and ventured his opinion on any subject. He had been watching the smoke for some time, engaged in deep speculation.

"Well, Uncle Pius," inquired Mr. Howard, "can you tell from the smoke what has been burning over at Bowen's place?"

"Kindar b'l'eve I kin," replied the old negro. "I suppose it am de old fellar's corn-crib, for de wood am green. You knows it ain't been up long."

"Could you tell from the smoke how much corn was in the crib?" asked the farmer.

"Jest what I'se been a ca'kalatin' on. Dar ain't much corn in dat crib, 'caze corn, it don't make no smoke like dat."

"How do you know?"

"I knows dis way, boss. Once when I'se a dryin' apples in de big stove, an' was a thinkin' 'bout som'in' or uddar, I'se dumped a bushel ob corn in de fire in place of de corn cobs. It made the funnies' sort ob smoke you ebber seed. Dat ain't no corn smoke; dat's wood smoke ober dar at ole Bowen's house."

"Now, we'll see if you are right," said the farmer. "If old Bowen has lost his corn, he'll let every one know it before night."

"Dat he will! Dat he will, sure! Den you'll see I'se ca'kalated right."

Mr. Howard laughed, and went into the house to take his breakfast. He was still anxious about Owen, fearing that some accident had befallen him.

Behind him walked Uncle Pius, muttering to himself: "Dar ain't much corn; dar ain't no corn in dat dar crib. Dar ain't—ain't—ain't."

CHAPTER V.

Owen and Martin Meet
Old Friends, and Owen Shows
How He Can Use a Rifle.

OWEN AND MARTIN trudged along the river bank for some minutes without uttering a word. Just as they were crossing a ravine, a large fox-squirrel sprang upon the trunk of a tall oak and ran to the top of the tree, which was so high that any but a practised eye would have looked for the animal in vain. After a short but careful search Owen discovered the bushy tail, and, changing his position a little, could see the squirrel looking down at him from its dizzy height. More for the sake of breaking the monotony of the walk than for the value of the squirrel, he raised his rifle and fired. There was a slight buzzing noise, and the ball fell on the ground in front of him.

"Powder wet!" he exclaimed. "That's what the rain does for a fellow's rifle."

"I had better try mine," said Martin, at the same time cocking his rifle and discharging it without raising it to his shoulder. "All right!" he continued, as the clear, sharp report echoed back from the cliffs.

"Halloo, youngstars! Any turkeys up in that there tree!" exclaimed some one from the top of the hill.

The boys looked up and saw Jolly Jerry. They had met the old trapper before, and were glad to find that they were not alone in the forest.

"No!" answered Owen. "It's only a fox-squirrel. I was trying my rifle."

"You are early this mornin', boys," said Jerry, coming down the hill.

"We were out all night," replied Martin.

"You was! I reckon you was almost frozen," replied the trapper. "Did you sleep under a tree?"

"We did at first; but it soon began to rain, and we went up under—under the—the bluffs," answered Owen with some hesitation, little dreaming of the importance of the answer.

Jerry put several other questions to see whether either of the two boys would say anything about the cave. But now that they were on their guard, they answered promptly and evasively. Jerry was satisfied—to press them farther might lead to suspicion; he therefore terminated the conversation abruptly, and began to look among the branches of the tree for the squirrel. Owen offered to point it out to him, but he motioned the boy aside, adding that he had not trapped in the forest twenty years for nothing. He continued his search for ten minutes, shifting his position continually. "Boys," he finally asked, "are you dead sure thare's a squirrel in that thare oak?"

"Yes, sir," said Owen, "just where it was when I first saw it."

Jerry looked a second time; much to the amusement of the two boys, he was again unsuccessful.

"Youngstars!" he concluded, "if thare's a squirrel in that thare oak, I'll eat him—bones, hair—and all, sure as my name's Jerry the Trapper."

"Wait until I load my rifle," said Owen, "and I'll bring it down for you." He had already dried his rifle, but could not use his powder, for the water had penetrated into the horn.

"Now I am ready," he continued, having used some of Martin's powder and loaded with great care; "do you want it barked, half-barked, or shot through the head?"

Owen's terms may need a short explanation. Frequently when a squirrel was in a high tree, with only a leg or a bushy tail visible among the thick branches, the huntsman could judge its position, and aim in such a way as first to pierce the bark and then the squirrel; this was called half-barking. But if he sent the ball under the squirrel, and killed it by the force of the shock without drawing blood, it was called barking or whole barking.

The trapper, who was not a little surprised at Owen's liberal offer, answered in his brusk, good-natured way: "Not partic'lar, youngstar, not partic'lar."

"Mother always prefers them shot through the head; she says that they are better when they bleed as soon as they are killed," said Owen.

"That's where we disagree; I'll take the feller barked. Bark him, youngstar, bark him if you can," said Jerry, at the same time getting in position to shoot the squirrel after Owen had fired, for he was convinced that only a champion marksman could touch it at such a height.

"I reckon I've got to eat him—hair, bones and all!" exclaimed the trapper, as the report of the rifle died away and the squirrel came tumbling through the branches of the oak.

"Did it touch a hair?" said Martin, holding up the squirrel and showing it to the astonished trapper. This was followed by a prolonged whistle from the latter, who continued for some time to examine the squirrel carefully, scarcely crediting the evidence of his senses.

"It's all luck! huntsman's luck! comes once in a lifetime! just like settin' a dead-fall for a weasel and catchin' a wildcat! I only seen it done once," expostulated Jerry. "Youngstar," he continued, "do you see that yeller-hammer off yonder through them there bushes?"

"Yes, sir," said Owen, looking in the direction indicated.

"If you send a ball through his right eye I'll eat him whole—head, feathers, and all."

"That's a hard shot," replied Owen. "The bushes are thick; then, besides, a yellow-hammer can't keep in the same place long enough for one to take aim. Look at it; its head is moving as fast as the spindle of a spinning-wheel."

"Try it, Owen," put in Martin. "I have seen you make harder shots than that."

While Owen was loading his rifle, the yellow-hammer flew, passing over the head of the trapper. Up went his rifle—crack—and the bird fluttered to the ground.

"I reckon you can't beat that, youngstars!" exclaimed Jerry, with evident satisfaction. "I've been practicin' for the shootin'-match next month. I ain't been there since Coon-Hollow-Jim, as they calls him, is been takin' the prizes; but I am goin' to out-shoot him, sure as my name's Jerry the Trapper."

"It would take a good marksman to beat that shot you just made," said Martin.

"That it would! that it would!" said Jerry, evidently pleased with the compliment.

"Owen, here, can shoot on the wing," continued Martin. "I've seen him"—here Martin paused for a moment, then added: "I've seen him hit them now and then." For Owen, too, had been practicing for the shooting-match to which Jerry referred. It was, as yet, a secret, however, which had been confided to no one but Martin.

"I say, youngstars, has you seen any notice of the shootin'-match?" inquired Jerry.

"No, sir," said Owen, "and I passed the cross-roads yesterday."

Jerry had accomplished his mission by detaining the boys for nearly half an hour, and, as they were anxious to continue on their way homeward, he parted with them without further display of his prowess with the rifle.

"Good mornin', youngstars," said he, putting the squirrel into his game sack and starting down the river. "I'll keep part of my promise by making my dinner on this here feller."

"Good morning!"

"Good morning!" said Owen and Martin almost simultaneously.

When Jerry had gone some distance down the river he turned and yelled to the boys: "If you meet my friend Stayford, tell him he'll find me near old Bowman's shipping place!"

"Why didn't I ask him about that dead-fall?" said Owen, looking down the narrow path where Jerry had disappeared.

"What dead-fall?" inquired Martin.

"One that will catch weasels and foxes. A weasel has been stealing our chickens every night."

"And can't you trap him in the ordinary dead-fall?" asked Martin.

"No! he is too sharp for them. The common dead-fall is good enough for wildcats and wolves. All that you need then is a heavy beam of wood, supported by a smaller piece, to which the bait is fastened; but this is too clumsy for a weasel, for he can make his escape before the trap falls."

"If we meet Stayford we'll ask him how Jerry fixes his small traps. I have caught foxes, but always used the long box-trap."

"I captured a weasel about two weeks ago," said Owen, "and what do you think he did? Gnawed his foot off and escaped."

While the boys were conversing about the sly little marauder of the chicken-coop and planning its destruction, they were hailed by Walter Stayford. He affected surprise to find them out in the woods so early, then questioned them as Jerry did, and received the same answer. The boys on their part had no suspicion of his being the man whom they had met in the cave, as it was too dark for them to see his features when he first appeared there. At Owen's request, Stayford explained how Jerry constructed his dead-falls for minks, weasels and other small rodents, whose skins possessed a market value. Instead of the one large log used for crushing the animal to death, he substituted four smaller ones, arranged parallel to each other, and about two inches apart. The trigger which supported these logs did not consist of a single strip of wood, but of three thin pieces shaped like the figure four, the bait being at the end of the horizontal piece and directly under the center of the dead-fall. The trigger thus set was very delicate, and fell if it was but slightly touched.

When Stayford had explained to the boys how to construct the trap he pushed on toward the place which Jerry had appointed for their meeting.

"Ha, ha!" he laughed to himself, as he walked along; "that was my plan, and it worked like one of Jerry's dead-falls."

It was indeed a good scheme to ascertain whether or not the boys would divulge the secret. No sooner had they left the cave than Jerry, who had already donned his hunting coat and cap, passing out into the forest by one of the secret entrances, and making a detour through the wood, reached the path about a mile up the river. Here he entertained the boys until Stayford could gain the path still farther up the Beech Fork. For this reason he pretended to look for the red-squirrel, and proposed to devour it whole if Owen succeeded in bringing it to the ground.

When Jerry and Stayford met they congratulated each other on the happy success of the ruse by which they had just tested the veracity of the two prisoners whom they had restored to liberty.

"They're all correct," said the trapper. "They ain't none of your gray foxes what one hound can ketch; but genuine red foxes, what can't be cornered by a whole pack."

"I watched them closely while I questioned them," said Stayford, "but not a word they uttered, nor any expression of their faces could give a clue to the fact that they were in the cave."

Returning to their underground home, the two men secured the rock door, threw themselves upon their beds of straw, and were soon fast asleep.

The boys hastened homeward, discussing excitedly their strange adventure so long as their way permitted them to go together, and even when their paths separated, Martin's following the river, and Owen's leading over the hills, their thoughts were much the same. Was there connected with that cave a secret which they did not know? Did this dark, weird, treacherous cavern shelter beneath its gloomy arches some strange occupant? They felt that there was a mystery in the history of the cave yet to be revealed.

CHAPTER VI.

A Visit From Father Byrne.

JUST AS OWEN entered the yard the dinner-horn blew, so he was forced to go at once to the dining-room. With his best efforts he could not conceal his drowsiness; he appeared somewhat frightened, too, and was naturally questioned about the previous day's hunt. His parents were surprised to find that the two boys had remained in the forest during a rainy October night. When did the rain commence? How long did it last? Was it cold during the night? Was Owen feeling well? The questions came faster than he could answer; they were of such a nature, too, as would likely lead Owen to commit himself and mention something about the cave. Luckily for him, however, the attention of the family was diverted to another subject by a little comedy which was just then enacted in the kitchen, where the negroes were at dinner. Wash, who was facing the road which ran in front of the house, suddenly sprang to his feet, upset his plate, spilt his glass of milk, and yelling as only Wash could yell, rushed from the door.

"Dat negro am jest as crazy as a June bug," remonstrated Uncle Pius. But he had scarcely uttered the words, when he, too, dropped his knife and fork and followed Wash. The other two negroes joined in the race; and one of them, Mose, tripping his companion, sent him sprawling in the dust. Bounce and Frisk now appeared upon the scene, running far ahead of the others, and shaking their tails in a friendly manner. Bertha and Owen sallied forth from the dining-room, waving their colored handkerchiefs above their heads, while Mr. and Mrs. Howard walked out upon the porch to welcome Father Byrne, whose arrival had caused the uproar.

Thus was Father Byrne received at the home of Mr. Howard. It was impossible to convince the negroes that they were too noisy on such occasions, for in their opinion the one who yelled the loudest gave the most hearty welcome. As the good priest seemed to enjoy their demonstration of affection, Mr. Howard never interfered.

Father Byrne insisted on partaking of the humble family meal, nor would he permit anything special to be prepared for him.

"I see you have a young stranger with you," said he,

looking across the table, where a little boy about two years old was propped up in a high chair.

"Not a stranger, Father," replied Mrs. Howard, "not a stranger. He's one of the family—Robin Howard is his name."

"Our children have all left us except Bertha and Owen," spoke up Mr. Howard. "Little Robin had no home, so we concluded to make him our boy."

"Ow'n and me go rid'n on ol' Hickory," interposed this youthful member of the family, whose chief delight it was to be lifted up on the back of old Hickory and to ride down to the water-trough.

"Can you ride alone?" inquired the priest.

"And the ol' duces (geese) went su–su–su–su."

"Why don't you answer the Father's question?" said the wife. "He wants to know whether you can ride alone."

"And the little duces went cry–cry–cry," said Robin, evidently trying to describe his encounter on the previous day with the flock of geese and goslings, in which encounter the little belligerent was evidently worsted, for one of the oldest warriors in the enemy's camp overthrew him with a single blow of his wing, and would no doubt have inflicted serious wounds had not Bertha come to the rescue.

"And what did Robin say?" asked Bertha.

"He cry, too," came the unwilling answer, whereat all laughed except the little soldier who had been vanquished in so inglorious a battle.

"Where is Owen?" asked Father Byrne, seeing that he had not returned to the dining-room.

"Probably he is not feeling well," said his father. "He and Martin Cooper were hunting wild turkeys all day yesterday. Toward evening Bounce trailed a large deer, bringing it near Rapier's Ford, where the two boys waited until they were overtaken by the night, and forced to sleep in the woods."

"Then I am not surprised that he is unwell," replied the priest. "Perhaps he will not be able to ride around to the different houses and let the people know that I am here."

"Then we'll give the work to Robin," said the farmer, with a laugh.

Robin, however, did not respond to the invitation. He did not seem to know that his name had been mentioned, but sat there in deep thought, planning the second and more successful campaign against the "duces."

"Well, Father," said Owen, riding up to the door just at this moment, "I had better be on the way, if I want to visit all the families before night, to let them know that you are here."

"They tell me that you are unwell," was the kind reply.

"Nothing the matter with me! Only a little stiff from sleeping out in the woods last night!"

"Of course, you'll never own up that you are sick," said his mother.

"Why should I own up, when I am not sick," said Owen; "besides, the ride will only do me good."

"If you do not feel strong enough to visit all the houses," said Father Byrne, rising from the table and walking out upon the porch, "return home, and let some of the other boys go in your place."

"Ow'n, dim me ride?" said Robin.

"Won't you come and finish your dinner before starting?" asked his mother.

Owen did not hear either appeal, however, but galloped away, only too anxious to escape from the company and the many questions about his night's experience.

Toward evening many of the Catholics came to the house for confession. Master and slave, old and young departed with the priest's blessing of peace, each holier and happier than when he came.

With patient care Father Byrne taught the older negroes their catechism; they, in turn, were told to teach their children. This was also a duty which he imposed upon the masters of slaves. To encourage the young blacks Father Byrne gave little pictures to those who had learned their prayers the best. It was on such occasions that Aunt Margaret endeavored to show the mental prowess of Wash.

"De Lawd bless dis negro," she said one day, "if dat Gawge Wasenton Elexander Hamilton Howard ain't got his skull as brim full of brains as ole massar's corn-crib is full ob corn."

"How long did it take him to learn 'Our Father,'" inquired the priest, much amused at the old negress' talk.

"Dat our foddar," continued Aunt Margaret. "Why, bless my soul! I gave him the first susposishin (explanation) of dat dar prayer last Christmas, and dat little negro he knowed it in less dan t'ree shakes of a sheep's tail."

"How many days?"

"No days, nuffin'. Bless him little soul, if de chile didn't larn dat our foddar in six mon's after I gave him the first susposishuns."

"Call him," said the priest, "and let us see whether he has learned his lesson well."

Washington came, and, standing before the priest with his hat on his head, began to recite the prayer.

"What I tole you do?" exclaimed his preceptress.

Off came the hat.

"Git on you' knees, you little her'tic!" again cried out Aunt Margaret.

Washington obeyed orders, and recited the prayer. He was rewarded by a picture, made thrice acceptable by its bold shades of red.

The Sunday following Father Byrne's arrival was bright and genial. The red-bird chirped among the crimson foliage of the maple; the blue-bird twittered and frolicked on the swaying branches of the plum-tree; round and round flew the barn-martins, as if they divined the coming winter, and wished to enjoy the few remaining days of autumn before departing for their more Southern homes; the swallows, too, with their speed-trimmed wings, darted swiftly through the heavens, glided noiselessly in among the trees, or sailed away again to the blue void beyond. A steady breeze sprang up, making the corn-stalks rustle in the fields, and sending the frost-nipped leaves of the forest whirling to the ground. Then, as the sun rose over the hilltops, the river lifted its white canopy of fog, slowly extended it over the valley, and dispersed it in fleecy clouds.

Along the several roads and footpaths which verged toward Mr. Howard's could be seen the members of Father Byrne's scattered flock hastening on to enjoy the rare privilege of assisting at Holy Mass.

"Good morning, Hez," said the host to Farmer Cooper, who was the first to arrive.

"Good morning, Zach."

"Fine morning."

"Very fine morning, indeed."

"How are you feeling?"

"Tol'ably well."

"How is Mrs. Cooper?"

"She's tol'ably well."

"And all the family?"

"They are all tol'ably well, thank you. And how are you this morning, Zach?"

"I am tol'ably well, thank you."

"And Mrs. Howard?"

"She is tol'ably well, too."

"And the rest of the family?"

"All tol'ably well, tol'ably well."

"How are you getting along with the fall wheat?"

"I reckon we'll be a little late this year," replied Mr. Howard. "It's the first time we've used the field for wheat, and have tried to get out as many stumps as possible. And how is your wheat getting along?"

"Tol'ably well. I reckon if nothing happens I'll have a fine crop next summer."

"What do you think about the fire over at old Bowen's?" asked Mr. Howard.

"I don't know what to think, Zach. This is the third time the poor fellow has lost his corn-crib. Just why the corn-crib should burn every year I don't understand."

"I reckon the negroes must set it on fire. They say he is very cruel toward them."

"I don't believe they burned his crib, Zach—I don't believe it. I tell you, there's something wrong with old Bowen, and some day or other we'll find it out."

While they were discussing the loss which old Bowen had sustained, and its probable cause, the Yates family arrived in the large farm wagon. Then came the Boones and the Blandfords, the Gates and the Craycrofts, and all the other Catholic settlers; and there was such a shaking of hands and exchanging of "good morning," and everybody was "tol'ably well," and was happy to find that his neighbor was "tol'ably well."

After Mass the same good wishes were exchanged, the same subjects of conversation rehearsed. Each one told just how much corn he expected from his summer crop, how much wheat he had planted for the coming season, the quantity of wool which his fold had yielded. The housewives, too, had their little stories to repeat. Each one knew how many sacks of dried apples her neighbor had stored away for the winter, how much apple-jam or peach-leather had been made. This, too, was the time for shy lovers to meet, and there beneath the great oak-tree, in rustic simplicity, many a vow was made and many a promise given.

The children did not accompany their parents home. Most of them remained at Mr. Howard's to be instructed by Father Byrne. When they had been dismissed, with the injunction to return for catechism on the two following days, the priest, accompanied by Owen, rode around to visit the sick who were unable to attend Mass that morning.

CHAPTER VII.

Mr. Howard Is Surprised by a Visitor—Owen Hears of the Great Shooting Match.

A FEW MINUTES after Father Byrne had left the house to visit the sick of the neighborhood a man rode up to the yard gate and called out, "Halloo!"

Mr. Howard, who was sitting on the front porch reading a book which Father Byrne had brought, looked up, and to his surprise saw before him Louis Bowen. The two men had been neighbors for fourteen years, yet they had exchanged but few words; not once during this entire period did Louis Bowen enter the Howard house. As he did not on this occasion dismount from his horse or seem inclined to come nearer, Mr. Howard walked out to the gate to meet him.

"Good morning," said he, approaching the visitor.

"I have been robbed, Howard! Burned out! Lost four hundred bushels of corn!" ejaculated Bowen, without seeming to notice Mr. Howard's welcome.

"I saw the fire early Saturday morning, but it was only to-day that I learned that your corn-crib was burned."

"The thieves first broke into my house, stole a small sack of money, and then set fire to my crib—my new crib, too, and full to the top."

"Truly unfortunate."

"The third time that my crib has been burned!" continued Bowen, growing more enraged.

"And it was full of corn each time, was it not?" inquired Mr. Howard.

"It was, Zach," said the sufferer, with a terrible oath. "Brim full to the rafters! The dogs waited until I had worked like a slave, and then in a single night they destroyed all that I had made!"

"And have you no clue to the thieves?"

"None at all! This it is that brings me here to-day, Zach! I want your help! I cannot track the rascals alone; this I have tried to do for three years, but without success. I have sneaked up and down the river, looked into the shipping stations, watched the 'arks' and flat-boats when they were being loaded, but found nothing! The State is full of hungry, lazy dogs, who do nothing but steal and live on other people's work."

"It is very strange," replied Mr. Howard. "I've been in this settlement for fourteen years, and as far as I know have not lost an ear of corn or a single potato. I really can't account for your loss."

"The thieves are not from this place, Howard! Starving dogs who rob and then burn what they cannot carry away! Many of the poorest people of the neighborhood come here to your house for prayer-meeting. I suspect some of them—I tell—"

"Louis Bowen!" interrupted the farmer, "every one of them is an honest man. If you accuse them of stealing, and cannot prove your words, I'll club you as sure as my name is Zachary Howard!"

"See here, Zach," said the cringing coward, who was not prepared for such a reception, "I didn't come here to fight. I came to ask your assistance in catching the thieves."

"The thieves, if there are thieves, are on your own farm—those poor slaves, whom you treat as beasts. Let me tell you, Louis Bowen, every man in this section of the country is talking of your cruelty toward those poor negroes!"

"That's my business, and not yours!"

"Then, if it's your business, don't come to me about it."

"So you refuse to help me to track the thieves?"

"I have given you my opinion on the subject, and I repeat now what I said—treat those negroes as if they were human beings, and you will have no further cause of fearing thieves and fires."

"I am not here to be insulted or dictated to. Again I ask, will you give me any assistance in this matter?"

"I have said all I have to say upon the subject. I have nothing else to add."

"Then let me tell you, Zach Howard, before we part," said the angered visitor, riding away at a safe distance from the man whom he was addressing, "I'll track those thieves alone, and when I find them, white or black, I'll—I'll treat them in such a way that all this country round will wonder that man could be so cruel and heartless." Going a little further on, he shook his fist at Mr. Howard and shouted: "I'll turn Indian, and burn them at the stake!"

Old Bowen departed. The farmer returned to the place where he had been reading, but he could not read. He was anxious and troubled. He felt that there was something more than a fire and a robbery connected with this visit, but what it was he could not divine.

In the meantime, Father Byrne and Owen had visited the different houses and were returning home, when they came to a place where two roads intersected. Here Owen's attention was attracted by a notice posted against a large oak-tree. It was evidently written by one who knew more of rifle-shooting than of the rules of orthography. It ran thus:

> *The Grate kintuckky rifle-shootin' for the fall Season will be on grundys Farm saterday, november 2, at hafe pass two in the Evenin'.*   *Nic Officar.*

"Just what I've been waiting for!" exclaimed Owen.

"Why? Do you intend to compete?" asked the priest.

"Yes, Father," was the reply. "Martin Cooper was there last year, and he says that I can shoot better than Coon-Hollow Jim."

"And who is Coon-Hollow Jim?" interrupted Father Byrne.

"Coon-Hollow Jim!" repeated Owen. "Why, I thought that everybody knew him! He is the best marksman in twelve miles from here, in a place called Coon-Hollow. They say he is about six feet and a half high."

"And do you think you can shoot better than such a man?" asked the priest, who was amused at the boy's earnestness.

"Martin told me that I could. Besides, I've been practicing for nearly a year. If you only help me, I think that I have a chance for the prize."

"How can I help you?" inquired the priest.

"By asking mother to let me go to the shooting match. She may think that I'm too young. But if you ask her, she'll be sure to let me go."

"Well, then," said Father Byrne, "since you are so anxious, and have been practicing for such a long time, I'll ask permission for you."

"Thank you, Father. To-morrow Martin and I will catch robins; then we'll go out and practice every evening until the day of the shooting match."

"It will be something like the fight between David and Goliath," said the priest. "I would like to be there myself to witness the battle. But now, Owen, you will have to ride in silence while I say a part of my office."

Father Byrne was not unfrequently in the saddle from morning till night, visiting his scattered flock. He rode a trusty animal with a quick and easy gait, and by long practice, could recite his office with as little inconvenience when traveling as when in his room.

Not wishing to disturb him, Owen rode ahead several paces. Twice he glanced furtively behind him. The good Father seemed lost to all around, and to have his thoughts fixed only on heaven, so that Owen wondered and wondered how he could pray so long and fervently. Half an hour passed. Again Owen turned, and saw that Father Byrne had dismounted and was kneeling. As he knelt there upon a moss-covered root, a sunbeam stole through the golden and crimson foliage of the forest and rested like a halo upon his face. Shadow and sunshine checkered the gay, leafy carpet which nature had spread out around him. The foxglove and wild bergamot, yet untouched by the frost, offered their fragrance in unison with his prayers, while bough and leaf which canopied him stirred not, as if unwilling to break the holy silence. And again Owen wondered and wondered how Father Byrne could pray so long.

"Father," said Owen, when the priest had rejoined him, and the two were again riding along together, "since you can't come with me to the shooting match, perhaps you would like to see me try my rifle at the house. I can bring down swallows on the wing; and they are harder to hit than robins."

"Bring down swallows on the wing!" repeated the priest. "Why, I never heard of any one doing that before."

"I once killed seven in succession," replied Owen, with no little satisfaction.

"You must get your rifle as soon as we return. I'll be satisfied with five swallows. If you kill five in succession, I'll acknowledge that you are a better marksman than Coon-Hollow Jim."

Shortly after returning home, Owen donned his cap and hunting-jacket, threw his powder-horn over his left shoulder, strapped his bullet-pouch around his waist, and sallied forth into the yard. He selected an open spot in front of the house, where he had a clear range in every direction, while Father Byrne, with Mr. and Mrs. Howard, stood on the open porch nearby. Robin, who was always frightened by the report of a gun, sought protection under a bed.

It was about half an hour from sunset. The swallows were flittering and diving through the air in quest of gnats and other insects, many of the birds passing not twenty feet overhead.

"Father," said Owen, adjusting his rifle for action, "we received a new keg of powder by the last stage, and I haven't had time to test its strength yet; so, if I miss the first few shots, you'll know the reason."

"No excuse! no excuse!" said the priest, with a laugh.

"If you do not kill five birds in succession, you are no match for the giant."

"Twit-r-r-r," and a swallow sailed by within ten feet of Owen's head.

"Twit-r-r-r-r," another had come and gone.

"Twit-r-r-r-r-r," and a third flew away unhurt.

"There!" exclaimed Father Byrne.

"There!" repeated Mr. Howard.

"I am waiting for one to come in the right direction," was the reply of the young marksman.

Soon one did come in the right direction. The rifle cracked, and the doomed bird fell to the ground with a flutter.

"Lo'd, dat's a shootin' boy!" exclaimed Mose, who just then appeared at the door of the negro cabin, and with this exclamation he began a lively jig on his fiddle.

"Twit-r-r-r-r,"—bang; and Wash, who had also appeared on the scene, ran for the second swallow.

Again the music started, again it was succeeded by the report of the rifle, and again Wash picked up the unlucky bird.

Owen waited for his chance every time. Six shots and six swallows were the results of the trial.

"Well, Owen," said Father Byrne, "you have more than surprised me. I predict success for you at the shooting match."

Even Mr. Howard was surprised at the deftness with which his son handled a rifle. He himself when young had been something of a marksman, but in his best days he had never equaled Owen. To kill six swallows in succession was almost marvelous. Prize shooters, even with sporting guns, could not bring them down with certainty; and when rifles were used, not one bird in ten was killed.

Rifle-shooting is an art. The marksman must know his gun, its exact range, the strength of his powder and exactly how much is required. Owen was not jesting when he told Father Byrne that he was not certain of his mark until he had tested the quality of his powder; this known, he could calculate the number of grains to use. Owen had one difficulty, however, which he had not yet mastered. In practicing he had observed that it was more difficult to kill a bird flying in a bee-line to or from him than one that flew to the right or to the left. When shooting swallows, he could wait for those which passed within the most advantageous range, but at the shooting-match he would be forced to take his robin as it flew from the trap. Owen resolved, with Martin's aid, to spend the following three weeks in overcoming this difficulty.

CHAPTER VIII.

Happy Days.

ON THE following morning the children were again assembled at Mr. Howard's for catechism. Those who lived within five miles of the farmer's house returned home at night, while others who were unable to come and go each day, stayed in the immediate neighborhood. Those were happy days for the dear little ones whom Father Byrne gathered around him. Prayers, instructions and lessons finished, the boys scampered off to the river to fish, or played "hide-and-go-seek" in the great hayloft, while the girls spent their happy hours in the grape-vine swings which Mr. Howard had made for them, or wandered out into the woods or into the fields to gather clusters of golden-rods.

No one enjoyed these days more than did Mr. and Mrs. Howard. They deemed it an honor and a privilege to have this troop of innocent children assembled beneath their roof. They insisted, too, on giving them a warm dinner each day, and supplying them with a bountiful repast before their departure. When the crowd began to break up in the afternoon (or rather in the evening, for the country folks of Kentucky never use the word afternoon), Mr. Howard was always there to see the children off safely. He took great delight in bringing their horses to the stile-block, in strapping on the blankets which they generally used instead of saddles, and in seeing them nestled snugly in their places, sometimes as many as four in a row on one horse. Then off they rode, laughing and talking, and saying a dozen goodbyes, and munching the biscuits and jam which Mrs. Howard had distributed among them. If the day was pleasant, the benches were brought out from the chapel beneath a large oak-tree near the house. Here Father Byrne heard the lessons and gave his instructions.

Early in the afternoon of the third day of class Mr. Howard came blustering into the room, and told Father Byrne to dismiss the children at once.

"I reckon, Father," said he, "we're going to have a heavy rain! Better get the children off at once!"

"Why do you think it is going to rain before night?" inquired the priest, with some surprise, walking to the door and surveying the heavens.

"Rain before night!" repeated the farmer. "Your reverence, it will be pouring down in less than two hours. Just look at that sun drawing up water. I tell you, if he keeps that up much longer, he'll have enough rain up in the skies to drown the country." Here Mr. Howard pointed toward the west to the long amber streaks, each one of which in his mind was a mighty pump supplying the rain-clouds from the distant ocean.

"I'll leave the matter to your judgment," said the priest. "It would be well to follow the more prudent course."

"You see, we shouldn't have room for them to stay over night," was the farmer's answer. "So I'll get the horses, and I'll start them at once."

There was a general murmur of disapprobation in the room, for the children disliked to disband so soon.

"Owen! Here, Owen!" yelled the farmer, going to the corner of the yard and calling his son, who was grubbing around the apple-trees in the orchard. "Come and help me to get the horses ready for the children!"

"Wife," he continued, appearing at the kitchen door, "can you get the little things something to eat? I am going to send them home before it rains."

"Why, dear," replied Mrs. Howard, "it has not been an hour since they had their dinner. And what makes you think it is going to rain?"

"The sun has been sucking up water now for some time. Just as soon as the sky is full, it will come pouring down."

"Well, the biscuits and chicken were cooked at dinner time. Aunt Margaret can have them ready in a few minutes," answered the wife, much amused at her husband's solicitude for the children.

"Great Jarusulum!" exclaimed the old negress in utter amazement, when ordered to get a lunch ready for the whole class. "Dem chilluns is goin' to eat up dis hole house, I know dey is!" for never in her experience had she seen such quantities of jam, biscuits and chickens disappear. In former years, the catechism class numbered about ten; this season it had more than trebled. Aunt Margaret began to fear that the whole tribe of chickens would become extinct, and when she went out in the morning to scatter food to the younger broods, she uttered words of prophetic warning. "You'se better hop off to de barn and get away from heah," she said, "for when dem chilluns is devou'd youse big brudders and sisters, dey'll be after youse, too."

While the lunch was being prepared, Owen and his father brought the horses to the front of the house. The latter again surveyed the sky, where the amber streaks had grown to twice their size, an evident proof that the sun was drawing up an unusual amount of water. This was a deep-seated conviction of the farmer, of which it was impossible to disabuse him.

"Owen," said he, "take these horses back to the stable."

"Don't you think it is going to rain?" asked Owen, in surprise.

"I don't think anything about it! I know it! It is going to rain pitchforks and millstones in less than an hour," said the farmer, emphatically.

Mr. Howard then stalked into the class-room, and told the children that they would all remain until after the rain—after the rain which would begin in about half an hour. The farmer proved a prophet; the rain came as he predicted, and at the time he predicted. It rained—it poured—it came down in torrents. Four, five, six o'clock, and still it rained, but this was not the only difficulty. The little creeks which crossed the road on either side of the house were swollen into rapid streams, which it was not only dangerous but impossible to ford.

"We shall have to keep the little ones with us," said Mr. Howard to his wife, when he saw that it was getting late and the rain had not in the least abated.

"And where can we stow them all away?"

"That's what I've been thinking about."

"You can send the boys home, and we can make room for the girls," suggested Bertha.

"It wouldn't hurt them to get a little wet, my dear, but I am afraid they cannot cross the creeks," replied the father. "I'll walk down to Cedar Creek. I can judge from it whether or not the fords are dangerous."

Mr. Howard's report was most unfavorable. Not even a strong man could pass to the other side of the stream without the risk of his life; it would be rash to let one of the children start home.

"Well, where can they sleep?" asked the wife.

"You take care of the girls," said the farmer. "I'll see that the boys live until morning."

"Oh, father! You are not going to put them up in the dusty garret!" expostulated Bertha.

"You and your mother see to the girls," said Mr. Howard, with a laugh. "I'll give you the whole house for their accommodation," and with these words he went out on the porch, where Father Byrne was talking with the children.

"What are you going to do with this little troop?" asked the priest.

"I went down to examine the creek, and found that it could not be forded. Even if the rain holds up awhile, which I don't think it will do, it will be impossible for any of the children to go home," replied the farmer.

A general burst of approbation went up from the crowd—the little girls danced, while the boys shouted and threw their hats into the air.

"Have you room for all of them?" inquired the priest.

"Room for the girls, I believe."

"Yes," said Bertha, who appeared on the scene; "we can put them all in the dining-room, and have a cover for each."

"Where are the boys going to sleep?" asked Father Byrne, turning to Mr. Howard.

"I have a much better place for them than Bertha has for the girls," answered the farmer, with a laugh.

"Where?"

"In the hayloft."

His words were followed by loud exclamations of joy from the boys, all of whom were delighted at the prospect of sleeping in the big hayloft. They had enjoyed their games of "hide-and-go-seek" there so much during the past days that it had become for them a home.

"I am going to find a good bed!" exclaimed one of the boys.

"So am I! So am I!" cried two others, and off the whole crowd went to burrow like so many rabbits into the heaps of oats and hay.

Aunt Margaret heard with utter consternation that her ravenous little guests were to remain until the morrow, thus demanding two extra meals to satisfy the cravings of their inordinate appetites. She groaned piteously when she reflected how many innocent chickens would be sacrificed to accomplish this end, and, following the instincts of self-preservation, she concealed a large ham in the chimney, lest she should die of hunger during the famine which must necessarily follow. Mr. Howard, however, saved the lives of the chickens by killing a sheep, which supplied the children with abundant repast.

Every effort was made by Father Byrne and the Howard family to entertain the children that evening. Father Byrne told them many stories of his missionary life in the almost uninhabitable sections of the State, where he was often forced to sleep in the open forest, with his horse tethered by his side. Once he was pursued by wolves, and was forced to abandon his horse to their fury. At another time, when in imminent danger of losing his life in a rapid current, he saved himself by grasping his horse's tail, and allowing the animal to drag him ashore. The priest interrupted his narratives at times to draw some beautiful and instructive moral for the children—how they should always trust in God, pray to Him in danger and temptation, and remember that their guardian angels watched over them day and night to shield them from all harm.

When Father Byrne had entertained the guests for an hour, Uncle Pius made his appearance with the other negroes, offering to serenade the visitors.

How they clapped their hands with joy at the announcement of such good news! Their eyes were fixed upon the venerable old negro as he tuned his fiddle and directed his assistants. Something was coming, something very funny! The music began. Uncle Pius rolled his large white eyeballs toward heaven in a most mysterious way; he twitched and screwed his face into every distorted shape; he knocked his knees together and struck the floor heavily with his big, broad foot; he whistled, he sang, he screamed, he shouted, until the whole house was in convulsions of laughter.

It was now growing late, and Mr. Howard announced that it was time for children to be in bed. They pleaded for one more song, which was granted. Then followed night prayers in common. Here no distinction was made between slave and master—all knelt to offer homage to God in unison.

"I'm scared," said one of the smallest of the boys, going to the window after prayers and looking out into the dark night.

"I tell you, it's dark outside," rejoined his companion.

"Say, do you think there'll be any ghosts in that barn to-night?" asked the first speaker.

"Don't know! Ghosts like barns, though."

"I ain't going!"

"Neither'm I!"

"Come on, boys!" cried the stentorian voice of Mr. Howard. "Come on! Let us be off to bed."

"John's afraid of ghosts!" said one of the boys.

"I am going to stay with you all night, boys, and leave the lantern burning," answered Mr. Howard.

This seemed to allay John's fears, for no ghosts, thought he, would ever venture where there was the least ray of light.

The barn was reached without accident, and the boys scrambled up the rickety ladder into their novel abode.

"Tom's in my bed."

"No, I ain't."

"I know you are. I know that's the bed I made!"

"What's the matter there, boys?" called out Mr. Howard.

"Tom Scott's in my bed."

"This is my bed, Mr. Howard," answered Tom, who by this time had burrowed deep into the oats, and had no intention of leaving his snug nest.

"Come up here, my little man," said the farmer. "I'll have a bed for you before you can say 'Jack Robinson.'" He then pulled two bundles of oats from the stack, and shoved the little sleeper into his improvised resting-place.

"Is everybody fixed for the night?" asked he. "We have two kinds of beds in this hotel—one of oats and the other of straw. You can have your choice, the cost is the same."

Everybody seemed contented.

"Well, go to sleep, boys! I'll be here with you all night."

Mr. Howard took a seat on an old barrel in front of the crowd. The boys were completely exhausted after their day's romping, and were soon fast asleep. Seeing that his services were no longer needed, the farmer threw himself upon the hay and followed their example.

On the following morning the children were dismissed immediately after breakfast. Father Byrne also took his departure; not, however, until he had encouraged David to prepare well for his coming battle with Goliath.

CHAPTER IX.

The Practice.

AFTER SUPPER on that same day, Owen left the house, and with a quick step followed a path which led over the hills through a large cedar grove. Here he mounted an old stump and gave a shrill whistle. No answer came but the distant echo. So he sat down upon the stump and began to mend a wide-mouthed sack, which he carried under his arm and which the mice had evidently been using for their habitation, having gnawed spacious doors and miniature windows in many places.

Every few seconds the prevailing stillness was broken by the whiz of myriads of wings, as flock after flock of robins settled in the deep glade for the night. It has been asserted by some naturalists that the robin is not a migratory bird. It is true that a few can be found in the thicket and barnyard during the winter months, but by far the greater number follow the swallow and blue-bird to warmer climes. Toward the latter part of autumn they pass through the Middle States, not by thousands only, but by millions. The thick cedar glades in central Kentucky were a favorite resort for them in their passage, and at night countless numbers roosted in the dark evergreen branches.

It was to secure a number of robins that Owen had ventured out. After repairing the sack with strips of elm bark, he again mounted the stump and gave another whistle. Soon Martin Cooper issued from among the cedars, at the same time waving a lantern above his head. He, too, carried a sack.

When it was quite dark, and the robins had settled down for the night, the boys crept stealthily along into the thickest part of the glade, carrying the lighted lantern. Now the fun began. Climbing a few feet up the trees and opening their sacks, Owen and Martin commenced to capture the affrighted robins. Many of the birds were so dazed by the light that they sat perfectly quiet, and were thrust into the sacks as easily as if they were apples hanging from a bough. Many, too, startled by the swaying branches, flew madly into the thicket, and by their cries spread the alarm throughout the evergreen domain.

Soon the whole glade was alive with the flutter and cries of the robins. Darting from tree to tree, they frightened those yet undisturbed. Robins screamed piteously. Robins yelled like street boys at the sound of the fire alarm. Old robins were demanding silence, and young robins were asking advice. Captured robins were fluttering in their prisons, and affrighted robins, dropping suddenly among the branches around the lantern, shared the fate of their doomed companions. Robins, robins, robins; singing, screaming, crying, laughing, up and down, back and forth they flew, until the sacks were filled and the boys departed.

An hour later all was quiet again among the evergreens. Old robins dozed quietly on the branches, while young robins on their first trip to the South dreamed of the rice-fields and orange-groves of the tropic zone. And still an hour later not less than four hundred captured robins, though imprisoned in a coop, dreamed that they were roosting among the cedars; while Owen and Martin in their snug beds dreamed of the shooting-match, and their future victory over Coon-Hollow Jim.

* * * * * *

"Helloo, Mart! What made you so late?" said Owen as Martin entered the field chosen as the place of practice.

"Late! It isn't late yet. You can kill many a robin before dark," answered Martin, at the same time putting down a box which he carried on his shoulder. "Here is the trap which I promised to make for you," he continued. "It works well, too. I had hard work in getting a good piece of wood for the trigger. That's what made me so late."

"Works nicely," said Owen, as Martin touched the trigger and the door flew open. "How many robins did you bring along?" inquired Martin.

"About fifty."

"That's as many as we can use. Now let's start to work."

Owen marked off the proper distance, while Martin put a robin in the trap for the first trial.

"Now I'm ready," said Owen, stepping up to the mark and raising his rifle.

As soon as the trigger was sprung the robin rose about six feet into the air, and then darted off directly in front of the boy. Almost at the same instant Owen fired.

"That'll never do," said Martin; "you didn't touch a feather."

"It's just as I told you," answered Owen; "I often miss them when they fly directly away. But let them go off one side, or in a half-circle, and they'll not escape so easily."

"Now for another trial," and Martin put the second robin into the box.

"What did I tell you!" exclaimed Owen, as his rifle cracked and the bird fluttered to the ground.

He then continued to shoot with varied success until it was so dark that his aim was no longer true.

Each afternoon he and Martin met at the same place for practice. During the first few days Owen failed in many shots, but toward the end of the third week, scarcely a robin flew from the trap that did not fall to the ground.

Besides Martin Cooper's practical assistance, Owen received no little aid in the way of interest and encouragement from his sister, Bertha. At evening, when he returned home after practicing, she almost overwhelmed him with a multiplicity of questions. "Are you improving? How many robins did you kill? How many did you miss? Do you think you will win? Oh, I hope you will! Don't you?" Thus she continued to ply question after question, and to interlard them with exclamations and surmises until she was forced to stop for want of breath. But Bertha did not content herself with words. In the woods she collected several kinds of bark used in dyeing, and made Owen a shooting jacket, resembling in some respects the many colored coat of Joseph. His old hunting cap was replaced by a new one made of the skin of a red-fox, with the bushy tail hanging at one side.

The weather remained clear for the next three weeks. The robins still tarried in the woods and thickets, rifling the elderbushes of their red berries, stealing the newly sown grain from the wheat fields, and at evening from bush and fence and swaying tree-tops caroling to the glories of the setting sun. They still sought their favorite haunts among the evergreen at night, where old robins again dozed quietly, and young robins dreamed of the sunny South; while in his snug bed Owen again dreamed of the coming contest with Coon-Hollow Jim.

CHAPTER X.

The Eventful Day.

"DO YOU THINK you'll win?" asked Bertha, as Owen mounted his horse and started off toward Grundy's farm for the eventful shooting-match.

"I don't know," was the answer. "I have done my part by practicing every day, and you have done yours by making me this gay coat, and by putting a new cord on my powder-horn."

"I only wish that I could do more for you— something that would win the prize."

"If I kill as many robins as I did in my last practice, it will be difficult to beat me," said Owen, taking the rifle which Bertha handed him, and balancing it on the pommel in front of him.

"And did you really bring down twenty birds in twenty shots?" asked Bertha.

"Certainly I did."

"And didn't miss one?"

"Not one! But why do you ask me that question? You heard me tell father all about it when I came home last night."

"I know that I did, Owen, but I wanted to hear you say so again. It makes me feel so much more certain that you are going to win."

"Well, if you are that easily pleased, I can repeat it half a dozen times."

"No! no! once will do! But, oh, me! I do hope you'll win," said Bertha, with a prolonged sigh.

"And so do I." With these words, Owen galloped off, while Bertha continued to repeat: "Oh, me! I hope you'll win! I hope he'll win!"

Owen was joined by Martin Cooper—generous Martin, who had encouraged him so much, who had been of such service to him during the three weeks of practice, and who was now accompanying him to the scene of the long-expected combat.

A large crowd had already assembled, and the preparations were gradually being completed. A rectangular space, measuring seventy by thirty feet, was marked off for the contestants. At one side was a platform for the three judges, and here those who wished to compete registered their names. The whole was enclosed by a temporary fence, strong enough to withstand the pressure of the crowd. This provision was necessary to preserve order, for as many as four thousand persons often assembled on such occasions. Some were so eager to witness these contests that they rode a hundred miles, and considered their two hours' enjoyment sufficient recompense for their two days of traveling.

The target was made of a thick piece of sheet-iron, one yard in diameter, and divided into thirteen rings of equal distance, gradually widening out from the center, called the bull's eye. It was considered a disgrace to go beyond number ten, and the one thus branded was expected to retire from the lists.

As each contestant stepped up to the platform to register his name, cheer upon cheer burst forth from the excited crowd. If he had won honors on a former occasion, his name passed from mouth to mouth, and he was welcomed back with loud and prolonged shouts.

"Hurrah—hurrah! for Poplar Flat!" cried a voice, as a long, gaunt and seedy looking fellow swaggered through the crowd. "Hurrah—hurrah! for Poplar Flat!" echoed a thousand voices. Now Poplar Flat was not the name of the individual thus welcomed. It was a low tract of land about thirty miles from Grundy's farm, and received its name from the fact that it was overgrown with large poplar trees. Its seedy representative was quite a favorite at the shooting-matches, and always answered his admirers by awkward bows, and three times throwing his cap into the air.

When he had retired, a heavy-set, low-statured contestant stalked up to the judge's stand. He carried his rifle with much grace, and registered his name "Green Briar." Green Briar was a rocky and barren locality, which produced nothing but briars, interspersed here and there with patches of sassafras bushes, and where the people, it was said, lived on blackberries and rabbits. The little rifleman, however, was not ashamed of his country, for he turned to the crowd and yelled at the top of his voice:

"Three cheers for Green Briar." Some inquired of him, in jest, if rabbits were plentiful, and if the blackberry crop had failed, while an old chum remarked to those around, "Look out for number one when that fellow raises his rifle."

All was suddenly hushed into silence as a young aspirant stepped into the ranks. Unlike the others, who gloried in their rude and almost wild costumes, he was dressed in what the country folks called "city style." His suit was not made of "home-spun;" he wore a felt hat, and his legs were cased in calf boots; both of which things were considered luxuries in the back woods of Kentucky. This remarkable personage was no other than the son of Old Bowen. It was simply to pose before the admiring crowd, that Charlie Bowen attended the shooting-match, for he had no chance of even a fair record in the contest; and from the way he held his rifle all could see that he was not accustomed to use it.

It was now Owen's turn to register.

"Courage, Owen, courage!" whispered Martin, as Owen left his side with a light but nervous step.

"Hurrah for the boy! hurrah! hurrah!" yelled a corpulent gentleman, who seemed to have an unlimited supply of lung power, and an unlimited stock of suggestions for applause whenever the cheering ceased. The motley crowd swayed to and fro, and seemed eager for applause, so the hurrahs were re-echoed until Owen reached the judges' stand.

Here, however, his youthful hopes were crushed. The oldest of the judges eyed him from beneath his black, overhanging eye-brows, and remarked in a dignified way that the contest was not for boys. Owen was a boy; a boy in age, in build, in appearance; if he entered the lists, he would have to enter as a boy.

"If the shooting-match is only for men," said he, "then, sir, I shall have to wait some time, for I am only fifteen."

"Fifteen!" growled the judge, forgetting his dignity, and again turning his dark eyes upon Owen. "Fifteen! why it would disgrace the whole contest, bring discredit upon the State, and, in fact, knock a hole through the entire 'riggar-mar-rang.'"

While the judge paused for breath after this spontaneous outburst of eloquence, Owen continued:

"Nothing was mentioned about the required age on the different notices posted in the neighborhood."

"Understood! understood!" cried the judge, waving his cane over his head, and then bringing it against the platform with such force that his two assistants started from their seats. "Why, at this rate, every impudent brat that owns a rifle would hand in his name, bullets would be flying around here in every direction, and there would be as many sons of America slain, as perished in the battles of Lexington and Bunker Hill. No, boy, you are too young; you cannot enter your name!" The judge was evidently pleased with this last attempt. He resumed his seat and gazed out over the crowd with much complacency.

Owen turned away with a heavy heart, and was about to leave the platform, when the jolly, corpulent gentleman cried out:

"Wait a moment, Judge! Give the boy a chance! Hurrah for the boy! hurrah! hurrah!" The crowd was not slow in joining in the chorus. Encouraged by the prolonged yells, Owen paused, although he could not summon strength enough to face the judge again. The yelling ceased; and while the stern judge deliberated whether he should abide by his iron rule or grant the crowd their wish, an old negro mounted a stump and began:

"Skuze me, Massar Judge, for 'sturbin' ob dis heah congregashun. But let dis niggar tol' you somethin'. Dat's de shootinest little feller ebbar you seed, and dis niggar will chaw his head off if he don't be de fust in de—de—de—" here he paused and racked his memory for a large word with which to end his climax. But the word would not come. So he commenced again:

"Ya! dis niggar hab seen him shootin', an' will chaw his head off if he don't be fust in de—de—de—" still the word refused to come, so the sable orator threw both arms above his head and leaped from the stump. His speech, however, gained the day; it was followed by peals of laughter and bursts of applause, and Owen Howard's name was recorded among the contestants.

Here several men galloped pell mell into the grounds. They had certainly traveled at no moderate speed, for their horses were spattered with foam, and, when the reins were drawn, stood panting like engines. The leader of the party dismounted, and shouldering his long deer-rifle, strode through the crowd with giant-like steps. What a picture of manhood! He did not appear to belong to the present generation, but rather to that race of ancient warriors, who wielded battle-axes, which men of our age can scarcely lift.

His disheveled hair reached his shoulders, his fox-skin cap was plumed with an eagle-feather, his deer-skin coat almost reached his knees, and his belt was made of the skin of a rattle-snake; while his dark moccasins completed his wild but attractive costume. He was pre-eminently the king of marksmen. Old and young elbowed their way through the crowd to catch a glimpse of this wondrous being; and from the time that Coon-Hollow Jim—for it was he—dismounted, until the judge called for the shooting to begin, his admirers yelled with unabated force.

CHAPTER XI.

David and Goliath.

ALL WAS NOW ready. The judge rising from his seat said in a solemn tone: "I have the honor, gentlemen, to announce the opening of the yearly Kentucky shooting match. As I am to address you at length at the close of the contest, I shall not now detain you by any inopportune remarks. I was going to remark that—but no—I'll not keep the crowd waiting longer. The men who are going to take part will please answer to their names when called by the director of the field."

The names of the participants were put into a box. To avoid delay two were drawn forth at a time; one firing while the other loaded.

Charlie Bowen was the first. The man at the target called out number thirteen, and the crestfallen humiliated youth disappeared in the midst of the crowd.

Poplar Flat's seedy representative sent two balls to number one, but becoming nervous at the third shot he struck the target between six and seven. Others then shot with varied success. "Green Briar" sent but one ball home—that is, to number one. The next two, however, grouping together in number three, made him the first among the twenty-six who had already fired.

Only two now remained, Owen Howard and Coon-Hollow Jim. So Father Byrne's prediction was verified—David and Goliath came forth to combat.

"Great pos-sim-mons! Youngster!" cried the old marksman, when he saw the size of his opponent. "You is a brave boy to fight a feller like me!" With these words he lifted Owen from the ground and carried him to the place of battle.

Since Goliath's name was called first, he stepped to the front, and raising his rifle sent the ball into the center of number one. Owen was encouraged by the giant's familiarity. He, too, was conscious of his power, so bringing his rifle to a level, with a true and steady aim he fired.

"Great pos-sim-mons!" exclaimed Coon-Hollow Jim, as soon as he heard the report of Owen's rifle. "She is not well loaded, or the powder is bad."

As these words were uttered the cry came from the target, "number nine."

Owen, too, noticed that his rifle had not its usual, clear ring. Seeing that he had shot so far from the mark, he knew that something was wrong. For months he had practiced at objects at the same distance as the target before him. Never had his aim been so untrue. The cause of his failure flashed upon his mind in an instant. Bertha had put a new red strap on his old powder horn. This was the first time he had used it since the night when he and Martin were caught in a heavy rain while returning from a hunt. The powder, he remembered, was then damaged. What was to be done? As Coon-Hollow Jim stepped forward for his second shot, Owen asked him for a few charges of powder. This was readily granted, and to the great surprise of all, the boy sent the next two balls to the center of the target.

Goliath "drove all three home." When the last shot had been fired the crowd rushed around him, raised him from the ground, and carried him to the platform in triumph.

A marksman in those days was held in high repute, and the champion at a shooting match was as jealous of his prowess as the crowned victor of the Olympic games. No honor was considered too great for him. We know from an episode in the life of Henry Clay, that, when candidate for the State Assembly, he once carried a whole district by a chance shot with a rifle.

Coon-Hollow Jim was now to receive the honors he had so well deserved. Seated on the platform with his long rifle in his hand, and the large eagle-feather dallying above his head, he listened to the eulogy pronounced upon himself, and the other heroes of America. For in the opinion of the speaker, Squire

Grundy, the marksman at his side was as great a hero as was Jefferson or Washington. The Squire was certainly a professional "stump speaker." Bombastic and incongruous words were strangely intermingled in his half finished sentences. Still he was never at a loss for a word. He spoke right on, whether there was sense in what he said or not. He needed no artful introduction to gain the attention of his hearers. So beginning with the discovery of America, he traced the progress of the country during Colonial days; dwelt at length upon the Revolutionary War, the battles of Lexington, Saratoga and Yorktown. Coming closer to his own day, he eulogized the great Admirals Hull and Perry, and added by way of parenthesis that he himself, Squire Grundy, had known the hero of Erie's battle. History unfortunately has preserved but a single fragment of his speech, though just where it was introduced the writer was unable to ascertain. "I am," said he, "a follower of the immortal Jefferson, the framer of our Constitution, and the pioneer of the human race." He concluded with a prayer for America's progress, and with much ceremony bestowed the prize, a silver mounted pistol, upon the champion marksman of Kentucky.

An intermission of thirty minutes was allowed the marksmen, while preparations were made for the second part of the program. In this each had twenty chances at robins, flying from a box at a distance of thirty yards. The "wing-shot," it is needless to say, was more difficult than target-shooting, and some who had acquitted themselves creditably during the first contest, withdrew their names.

Scattered in knots over the field, many were talking in a mysterious way. Some hinted that every one would be surprised except themselves. Others claimed that three of the marksmen who had held back during the target shooting, would bring down every robin which flew from the box. It was also rumored that two men, who had just registered their names, were marvels in the rifle-craft, that they had won prizes at every shooting-match in the United States; that one, who had large, owl-like eyes, could kill a swallow further than most men could see it. Jolly Jerry, too, was there, exchanging jokes with his old friends and making arrangements for the winter dances; he had not entered the lists thus far, but had reserved his prowess for a more signal battle.

Martin Cooper had not lost hope. Owen, he was convinced, had but one equal in the State, and had it not been for an unforeseen accident, he would have divided honors with Coon-Hollow Jim. In shooting on the wing he thought that his young friend was superior to any one on the grounds.

"Bad luck, Owen," said Martin, as the two met after the conferring of the first prize.

"All Bertha's fault," said Owen. "I had my new powder horn ready, and was about to start, when she came running out with this old one. Since she had gone to the trouble of weaving a new string, and of putting these yellow tassels at each end, I changed to please her. The powder in the old horn was damp, and this spoiled all that I put in."

"Too bad! wasn't it?" replied Martin. "But you have another chance yet, and I am sure you are going to show the crowd what you can do."

"Well, the powder is dry. I am certain of that. Mr. Lane, or Coon-Hollow Jim, as we call him, gave me half of his. He says it's the best made."

"So his real name is Mr. Lane," answered Martin, with some surprise. "Isn't he a good and kind fellow? He made everybody laugh when he carried you to the place for shooting."

"When I offered to pay him for the powder," continued Owen, "he tapped me on the head saying 'that's all right, my little man, I hope you take the next prize, but I am going to do all I can to get it myself.'"

"If you do win," said Martin, "it will be the whole story of David and Goliath, for you will use Coon-Hollow Jim's powder to beat him with, just as David used the sword of the giant to cut off his head."

"I shall do my best, Mart!" said Owen, "but, see, the men are getting ready. It's time for the second part."

"Now for work! Show them what you can do!"

CHAPTER XII.

Killing Goliath
With His Own Sword.

AFTER THE FEW preparations were completed, Squire Grundy again arose, and in a solemn voice announced the second part of the program.

Hurrah followed hurrah when Coon-Hollow Jim's name was the first to be drawn from the box, and the big giant stepped forth to win a second victory. How gracefully he swung his rifle from his shoulder! How true his aim! How telling was every shot! At one time he brought a robin to the ground before it had risen above the heads of the spectators; at another he let it sail so far away that to kill it seemed impossible. It mattered little which way they flew—to the right or left, up into the air, or directly from him—every shot was equally fatal. The marksman wondered at his own skill, for never before had he made such a record—twenty birds in twenty shots. How the crowd yelled! yelled louder and louder at each successive shot, until, at last, when the twentieth bird was killed, Coon-Hollow Jim was lifted from the ground and carried to the judge's platform.

After such an exhibition of rifle-craft, and such an outburst of wild enthusiasm, the shooting that followed was slow and uninteresting. Anyone who failed in a single attempt was forced to retire, since by this failure he forfeited all chance of winning a prize. The man with the owl-like eyes missed the first robin at which he fired; the seedy representative from Poplar Flat shared the same fate, while the noted marksman from Green Briar disappointed his numerous friends by letting the fifth bird escape.

Then came Jerry's turn. The reappearance of the jolly old fiddler at the shooting-match was of itself sufficient to revive the waning enthusiasm of the spectators. "Swing corners," shouted a voice from the crowd. "Balance all," yelled another, for the sight of Jolly Jerry awakened many pleasant recollections of summer picnics and winter dances. He killed the first bird, the second, the third; then the crowd became excited again. The hurrahs were almost as deafening as those which Coon-Hollow Jim received. In fact, the giant marksman became restive in his seat as he saw bird after bird fall before the steady aim of the old trapper. Then there came a silence. It seemed as if every spectator there was suddenly stricken dumb. Every eye was riveted upon an object which was slowly becoming but a small speck in the sky. It was the robin which Jerry had missed—not missed altogether, however, for the bullet had cut several feathers from its wings, so that it flew with great difficulty.

A horseman galloped after it in order to bring it back if it should fall. This would count, provided the bird could be placed in the trap before five minutes had passed. The robin sailed toward the ground, then into the air again; here it fluttered, sailed and fluttered again. Would it fall? Yes—no. It reached the woods, and was safe. Jerry gazed at the crowd as if soliciting sympathy, then turned toward Coon-Hollow Jim, brandished his rifle in the air, and said:

"I'm gettin' old now, an' my han's ain't steady, but there was a time when no man in this hare State could out-shoot Jerry, the trapper."

The men who followed met with but little success. Then came Owen's turn, the last of all. By this time the crowd was beginning to break, and many had already departed, so it was not under very favorable circumstances that our young hero came forth to make a name.

The trap flew open, the bird flew out, the rifle cracked, and down came poor robin red-breast.

"That's the last he'll get," said a tall man with a high voice.

But it wasn't the last. The next bird shared the same

fate; so did the next, and the next, and the next, until at last eight had fallen.

The crowd cheered—cheered so lustily that many who had started off turned in their saddles and looked around. Owen all the while was scarcely conscious of the surging crowd around him. He loaded his rifle rapidly, fired rapidly, loaded and fired again.

"Great pos-sim-mons!" exclaimed Coon-Hollow Jim.

"Hurrah! hurrah for the boy!"

"Hurrah for the boy! hurrah for the boy!" re-echoed the frantic crowd.

The excitement spread. The horsemen, who had reined up near the grounds, called to those in front of them. These in turn signaled to the moving groups farther on, until the alarm reached the bands that had first departed. What had happened, the different parties knew not. Certainly it was something extraordinary. So without exception each horseman put spurs to his animal and galloped back. When Owen raised his rifle for the last and crowning shot, a deathlike silence fell upon the spectators. But this silence was of short duration. The robin flew straight into the air, then wheeled around with a graceful curve—a sharp report, and down the bird twirled to the ground.

Martin all the while was standing apart from the crowd, watching Owen's every movement, confident of his power, yet dreading some possible accident. As the twentieth bird flew from the trap, he buried his face in his hands, nor did he dare look up until the wild cheers told that his friend had won.

Owen was nearly suffocated by the men who pressed around him. "Great pos-sim-mons! don't be a killin' of the feller!" cried Coon-Hollow Jim, who had left the platform and was standing close to the boy's side. With this expostulation he lifted Owen to his shoulder, worked his way through the crowd like an old crusader on the battle-field, and placed his charge on the judge's bench.

Squire Grundy rose to make a speech, but the crowd yelled him down, and demanded that the two heroes of the day should come forward again to test their skill. Owen's heart beat with honest pride as he stepped down from the platform and walked side by side with his giant opponent—still his warmest friend. Again David and Goliath came forth to battle.

Goliath was the first to fire; he killed his bird, but so did David; he brought down the second, but David also brought down the second; he killed the third, the fourth, the fifth; but David did the same. At each shot the mobile crowd swayed to and fro and reiterated its deafening cheers. Then there came another silence for, alas! Goliath had failed to hit the fluttering mark. The silence was prolonged, for each one seemed to hold his breath as he watched Owen's last attempt. Martin again closed his eyes and hid his face within his hands. He heard the sharp report of Owen's rifle, and then such shouts as he had never listened to before. The yearly shooting-match was over, and Owen Howard had made a record which was never before or afterward equaled.

Our little hero would certainly have been crushed to death had he not been rescued a second time by his giant friend, who again carried him to the platform, piled together the benches of the stand, and high above the heads of both the judge and people placed the youthful victor.

When Owen had received the glittering, long-coveted prize, Coon-Hollow Jim arose and demanded a hearing. He spoke of the years that he had used the rifle, of his many victories in different parts of the State, and concluded by frankly owning that he had met his superior. With this acknowledgment he removed the pistol-strap from his own waist and handed it to Owen, and upon his refusal to take it, despite all protestations, secured the belt around the boy's waist. Coon-Hollow Jim never again appeared at a shooting match.

Years afterward old men were wont to speak of this eventful day, when a youthful hero took the prize from the best marksman in the State.

CHAPTER XIII.

Bertha Hears the News of Victory.

THE NIGHT after the shooting-match was damp and chilly. Near the fire which roared up the spacious chimney in what was called the family-room, sat Mr. Howard whittling at a wooden latch for the kitchen door. Mrs. Howard was busy with her knitting needles, while Bertha kept the spinning-wheel in perpetual motion.

"It's getting late," said the father, as the old-fashioned clock above the mantel struck eleven. "We can't wait for Owen much longer."

"Oh, me! Let us wait, father! I shall not be able to close my eyes to-night until I've heard Owen tell all about the shooting match. I do just hope he will win! Don't you?" answered Bertha, and in her excitement she made the spinning-wheel buzz and screech.

"You have said that at least twenty thousand times

to-day," drawled out the farmer, as he cut a long shaving from the hickory stick in his hand.

"Yes! she has been wishing, and wishing, and wishing all day," remarked the wife.

"You don't know how I feel," said Bertha. "Oh! I just hope he'll win! I can't stand this waiting any longer!"

Here the conversation was interrupted by the barking of Bounce.

"Oh! there he is!" cried Bertha, letting the yarn drop from the spindle, and running to the door. "Owen! Owen! did you win, Owen? Owen, did you win?"

"What is all this excitement about?" inquired Father Byrne, as he dismounted from his horse and walked into the yard.

"Why, Father Byrne!" said Bertha, immediately changing her tone of voice, and addressing the priest with the greatest respect. "I thought you were Owen. He has been at the shooting match all day, and I do just hope he will win!"

"And so do I," rejoined the priest with a smile.

"Welcome! Welcome! Father," said Mr. Howard, who appeared at the door carrying a lighted candle.

"I am returning from a long sick-call," said the priest; "have been riding all day, without having anything to eat. During the last two weeks I have had three sick-calls of over sixty miles each."

"You must be tired indeed," said the kind farmer in a sympathetic way. "Sit down near this bright fire, Father. Bertha will soon have a warm supper ready."

"She will have to hurry," said the priest, "for it is past eleven. I'll take a short rest of two hours, and then be on my way again in time to say Mass."

Father Byrne had scarcely taken his seat when Bounce gave a second alarm.

Again Bertha ran from the house toward the yard-gate, exclaiming: "Owen! Owen! did you win, Owen?"

"Good evening," answered a strange voice.

"Where is he? Did he not come?"

"Your brother Owen will probably not be home to-night."

"Has anything happened?"

"No; but you do not know me?"

"Oh, do tell me the news, sir."

"I'm Walter Stayford."

"And were you at the shooting-match, Mr. Stayford? Did Owen win? Why won't he come to-night? Oh, do tell me."

"Nothing serious has happened," said Stayford, very deliberately. He had never visited the Howards, but had often met Owen and his sister at dances and picnics, so he felt that he was not altogether a stranger to Bertha. Her eagerness and curiosity provoked him to withhold the good news he had come to tell.

"But did he win? where is he?"

"We left him at Grundy's farm."

"Then you were there?"

"Yes."

"And you saw the shooting match?"

"Yes."

"And did Owen take part in it?"

"Yes."

"Oh, do tell me, sir."

"Good evening, Mr. Howard," said Stayford, turning toward the farmer, who had just then walked out into the yard in the full light of the blazing fireplace. "I have just been trying to tell this young lady all about her brother's victory; but she won't listen to me."

"Then he won," exclaimed Bertha, in boisterous glee.

"Yes—yes, he won—outshot the whole State."

"He can certainly handle a rifle," said the father.

"That he can. I reckon he'll never meet his equal."

"Well, I reckon too much praise will spoil the boy. But where is he?"

"Why, he stayed to take supper with Squire Grundy. It's customary for the winner, you know. He will probably not be back to-night."

"Won't you step into the house?"

"No, I reckon not," answered Stayford. "I'm waiting for Jerry. I rode ahead to bring the good news. You see, Owen beat Jerry, too; but the old trapper didn't care as long as Coon-Hollow Jim lost the prize. He's in Tom Barn's hay-wagon with Sisco, Bechem, Brown, Craycroft and half a dozen others. I reckon he's coming now."

Far down the road could be heard the notes of Jerry's fiddle.

Suddenly with a wild shout two horsemen dashed up. They were Martin and Owen. The latter had declined the Squire's invitation to dine; hence the boys had arrived sooner than was expected.

"So David returns with the head of Goliath," said Father Byrne, grasping the boy's hand.

"Yes, Father, I have won," replied Owen. "But to your kindness and Martin's help belongs more than half the victory."

Bertha was not there. She had gone away to weep for very joy.

CHAPTER XIV.

Brother and Sister.

AS OWEN was fatigued after so many hours of excitement and exertion, he remained in the house the greater part of the following day. This afforded Bertha an excellent occasion of hearing a full account of the shooting match. Owen had scarcely seated himself before the fire-place in the family-room, when his sister brought in her spinning-wheel, and began alternately to work the spindle and ask questions.

"Now, Brother Owen," said she, "do tell me all about yesterday—what happened, how you won—oh, just everything!"

"Buzz-z-z," went the spinning-wheel as if to say, "hurry on, Owen, hurry on, for your sister has many, many questions to ask."

"Did the people like the new cap and coat I made for you?"

Buzz-z-z.

"Did you hit the center of the target every time?"

Buzz-z-z-z.

"How many robins did you kill out of the twenty?"

Buzzz-z-z-z-z.

Buzz-z-z-z-z-z-z-z-z.

And Bertha talked so fast, and the wheel buzzed so loud, that Owen did not reply.

"Oh, it's just too mean to keep me waiting so long before telling me all about it!" said Bertha.

"I thought that wheel was answering your questions; you both talk at about the same rate," said Owen, playfully, for he saw that his sister was much excited, and wished to tease her by delaying to answer at once.

"Well, I saddled Log after breakfast, and—"

"I know you did," interrupted his sister; "do tell me something new."

"How can I if you stop me as soon as I begin to speak! Well, I saddled my horse, and took my rifle, and—wait, I forgot something! First, I put my powder-horn over my right shoulder"—a pause—"and then I put my bullet-pouch over my left shoulder"—another pause—"and then I took my rifle, and went down and saddled old Log, and started off, and—Oh, you've killed me! Oh! oh! oh!" For Bertha had taken a ball of yarn from a basket near the spinning-wheel, and playfully struck Owen in the head with the harmless missile. After this bold attack, a treaty of peace was signed, and Owen agreed to answer every question seriously and without delays. He was interrupted in his narrative by some one calling in a loud voice from without:

"Halloo! Halloo!"

It was Louis Bowen. Has he heard of Charlie's going to the shooting-match? was the thought which rushed to Owen's mind as he walked to the yard-gate, where the unexpected visitor was waiting astraddle his horse.

"Good-morning, Mr. Bowen," said he, with all the composure he could summon up.

"I hear you were at Grundy's farm yesterday," said the man gruffly, without seeming to notice Owen's morning greetings, "and I would like to know if you saw my son Charlie there. He hasn't returned yet."

"Yes, sir, he was there."

"The scoundrel!" muttered Bowen. "I'll flay him alive! He is getting worse every day. Spends money as fast as I can make it. I'll—I'll kill the wretch!"

"Many men camped on the grounds all night. He may have stayed with them," said Owen.

"I'll drive him from the house when he comes back! If he won't work, let him starve!" continued the father. "My corn-crib burned, my money stolen and squandered! Misfortune and losses on every side! I'll—I'll—but say, boy, you were along the river the night my crib was burned. Did you meet no one?"

"We met Jerry and Stayford the next morning, sir."

"Did you meet no one that night? Where did you stay that night?"

"We slept under the trees until it began to rain, and then—we went up the hill under the bluffs."

The conversation was here interrupted in a most singular manner. Charlie Bowen passed along the road, close to the two speakers. The father and son recognized each other at almost the same instant. Charlie spurred his horse and dashed down the road, while Mr. Bowen uttered a curse and started in pursuit. The scene was ludicrous in the extreme. Owen felt very serious and nervous while listening to the old farmer's threats, but now he forgot his troubles, and, mounting the gate-post to get a better view, watched father and son as they galloped along the dusty road. Still, when he reflected seriously, he could not but commiserate them both.

Returning to the house, Owen continued his lengthy description of the shooting-match, until Bertha's curiosity was entirely satisfied. During the following week, Bertha visited many of the neighbors, and repeated for them the history of her brother's victory. She also wrote an account of the contest for the Lexington paper and sent it by the stage which passed the house every second week.

Mr. Howard was not so enthusiastic over Owen's success. He was not a rigorist; he could not be called a severe man; still, he did not believe in spoiling children by humoring and flattering them. He feared lest the honors which Owen had received would exercise an evil influence upon him for the future, and felt it his duty to check any such influence at the start by keeping him at steady work.

"Owen," said he on the following morning, "you've had a whole day to rest, so get your axe and come with us to the woods. We must get that strip of land along the river cleared before winter."

After breakfast Owen shouldered his axe, whistled for Bounce and Frisk, and followed the workmen to the woods. The smaller trees were left for him to cut, while the men felled the large oaks, hickories and poplars. Day after day the work progressed. The steady stroke of the axe rang out clearly in the crisp, morning air, and the burning brush-piles dispelled the gloom of the autumn evenings. Occasionally some massive poplar of more than a century's growth would crash to the ground with a force that shook the earth for many yards around, tearing huge branches from the surrounding trees, crushing the smaller ones beneath its ponderous weight, and causing the hills on the other side of the river to ring with prolonged reverberations.

Owen enjoyed the work. He wielded his axe with a true and telling stroke. His hands and muscles were gradually hardened, until he could labor the entire day without the least fatigue.

At night when he returned from the woods he improved his mind by constant study and reading. Learning one day that a certain Mr. Rolling, who had come to the Howard's to buy some stock, was the happy owner of a wonderful book called "Robinson Crusoe,"

Owen was very anxious to make the acquaintance of Robinson, as he had often heard of his adventures on that far-off island. Mr. Rolling readily consented to lend him the book, promising to bring it to him at the first opportunity. The delay, however, was too long for the boy's impetuous nature; after waiting a few days, Owen decided to ride over to the farmer's house to secure the much-coveted volume.

"You have come after poor old 'Robinson Crusoe,' have you?" said Mr. Rolling, when he met the boy at the door.

"Yes, sir. It's a long ride, but I wanted to read that book, and determined to come after it at once."

"You are a funny, funny boy," replied Mr. Rolling. "And now I am sorry to tell you that you will have to ride five miles farther, for friend Foxway hasn't returned it. You see, old 'Robinson Crusoe' is quite a favorite in the neighborhood, and is continually traveling from one place to another."

"The ride isn't long," said Owen; "but perhaps Mr. Foxway has not read the book."

"Only him and his wife there. I reckon they know the whole story by heart. Tell Mr. Foxway that I sent you for the book. Why, it is worth a five-mile ride to get a look at the farmer and his wife."

Mrs. Foxway was certainly a curious little creature, with a withered face and weasel eyes. She received Owen very kindly, invited him into the house, and, when informed of the object of his visit, went at once to get the book. "Robinson Crusoe," however, seemed by no means desirous of making Owen's acquaintance, for Mrs. Foxway, after searching every room in the house, upsetting a table and breaking several pieces of china-ware, finally concluded that old Robinson had run away. She insisted, however, that he could not have gone a great distance, for her husband had him in his hands that very morning, while she was preparing breakfast. She informed Owen that Mr. Foxway would soon be home for dinner, and assured him that her husband was never known to misplace anything, and that if the book had not left the house of its own accord, he would find it the moment he came. She then returned to the kitchen to continue her work, and Owen was left alone.

"Here he is! Here he is!" screeched little weasel-eyes, soon after she had gone into the kitchen.

"Mr. Foxway has returned rather early," mused Owen. "But why should his coming create such excitement?"

"Hiding in the flour barrel! Hiding in the flour barrel!" called out weasel-eyes in the most alarming way.

"Hiding in the flour barrel!" repeated Owen to himself. "Perhaps he did not want to give me that book."

"Ha! ha! All covered with flour!" came the screechy voice from the kitchen.

"If he didn't want to give me the book, why didn't he say so," thought Owen.

"O mister! mister! Come and look at him before I dust him off with the turkey-wing," cried the little woman.

Owen started toward the kitchen expecting to find a wee little man sprinkled with flour, but Mrs. Foxway was the only one there, standing near a barrel, with the turkey-wing duster in her right hand.

"Trying to hide! Nearly covered with flour!" she said, pointing down into the barrel.

Owen looked in the direction indicated and was surprised to find, not the dwarfish farmer, but the book which he had come to get. It had fallen from the kitchen table into the flour barrel, and presented quite a snowy appearance. In one of the pictures where Robinson was sitting in his rude house, with his parrot on his knee, both were entirely embedded in the late mimic snowfall. Friday seemed to have forsaken his tribe, and become a Caucasian, for he was as white as his master. A few strokes of the dusting brush, and everything was restored to its original color and true form—the parrot became a bright green, while Friday, like the jack-daw, shorn of its stolen feathers, resumed his sable hue.

At last Owen had obtained the long-desired book. In its dilapidated condition, it appeared to have passed through as many catastrophies as old Robinson himself, not excepting the shipwreck, for some careless reader had let it fall into a bucket of water, on which account it had lost one of its covers and expanded to wonderful proportions. A whole category of Robinson's admirers had made use of that old-time way of marking the place, (often condemned, but more often practiced,) until almost every page was dog's-eared. Although these marks detracted from the appearance of the book, they by no means lowered it in Owen's estimation. On the contrary, he regarded it in the same light that he would a veteran soldier who had served in many campaigns, and whose reputation was enhanced by the number of wounds he had received.

Mr. Foxway now appeared upon the scene. He was even smaller than his wife—a big, round head, large, oval eyes, and thick duck-legs. He reminded Owen of the little screech-owls which often peered out at him from the dark eaves of the barn. The farmer was more than willing to part with the book, as he intended to return it to Mr. Rolling that afternoon.

Many a pleasant evening did Owen and Bertha spend in "Robinson Crusoe's" company. Moreover, the little screech-owls in the barn were ever afterwards called Mr. and Mrs. Foxway.

One night while Owen sat before the bright fire-place with the interesting volume in his hand he chanced to turn the pages, and there upon a fly-leaf saw some writing and a rough drawing which excited his curiosity. The writing was crude and scarcely legible; the drawing evidently represented a place or scene along the Beech Fork.

"What have you found?" asked Bertha, who noticed Owen's intense interest as he leaned closer to the fire to get a better light.

"Oh, nothing!" he replied with forced indifference.

"Let me see."

"You would not understand it."

"So there is something on that page?"

"Yes, but you could not make it out, for you never saw the—." Here Owen paused.

"The what?" asked Bertha.

Just then the book dropped from Owen's hands. The fly-leaf, which was loose, fell out, was caught by the strong draft of the fire-place, and was carried up the chimney.

"Oh, Bertha!" cried Owen. "There it goes, and it's on fire. It was all about a great secret, a—oh, if I could only tell you! But some day you shall know all about it."

CHAPTER XV.

Around the Fire-Place.

FATHER BYRNE, who had noticed Owen's fondness for reading and wished to encourage him in this respect, brought him the few books he could obtain. Among the number was a selection of English poets, the first book of poems which Owen had ever seen.

He had not possessed the treasure many days before Martin Cooper came over to see it. When the latter arrived, Owen was busy with the chores.

"Don't wait for me, Mart," said he. "You'll find the book on the mantel. I'll be through in a short time. I've some news, too, about the cave."

"Just as you say. I'm anxious to try that wonderful book."

Martin seated himself before the spacious fire-place, which served the double purpose of heating and lighting the room, and began his work of inspection. The book was opened at random, and a passage of Shakespeare read—a difficult one, not a line of which was understood. What could a farmer-boy who had read scarcely a dozen books expect to gather from the pages of Shakespeare? Martin closed the book, examined the cover, gazed into the fire-place, watched the shadows, and whistled three times. After this performance had been concluded, the book was again opened, but at a different place.

"Il Pen-se-ro-so"—he was forced to spell every syllable of the strange title, and as for the poem with its many mythological allusions, it was worse than a Chinese puzzle. Again Martin shuffled his feet, again he stared at the shadows. He then opened the book for the third time, with a firm resolve that if he did not understand the next lines he would never in the future enter the domains of poetry. Did his eyes deceive him? He leaned forward to get a better light. Was there really a poem on Kentucky? Impossible! He was dreaming! No, there it was, and to make sure that he was not deceived, he pronounced every letter, "K-e-n-t-u-c-k-y," and then read the line, "Kentucky's wild and tangled wood." Book in hand he rushed from the room into the yard, calling at the top of his voice: "Owen! Owen! here's a poem about Kentucky."

When the two boys returned to the room, they found that the poem was entitled "Marmion," the line,

"Kentucky's wild and tangled wood," being simply an allusion to their State.

"Halloo!" exclaimed Owen, examining the title page, "it's written by a fellow named Scott."

"From Scott county," suggested Martin.

"May be. He seems to know all about the country."

"Yes! He says it's wild."

"I wonder whether he ever saw 'Green Briar'? It's the most tangled part of the State I know of. I went 'coon hunting one night, and got so tangled up among the bushes and briars that when I came home I had only half a coat."

"Let us see what the book says about Scott!"

"He lives in England," said Owen, turning to a brief account of the author's life.

"Did he ever come to this country?" inquired Martin.

"No! At least there is nothing here about it."

The boys were disappointed, for they had at first concluded that the poem was about Kentucky, and afterwards that the writer himself was a Kentuckian. Scott, however, had mentioned their native State; so without a long process of reasoning they placed him first among the poets.

"Look at this," said Owen, pointing to the title of the first book of "The Lady of the Lake."

"What is it?"

"What is it! Why it is about a chase—a deer hunt."

The boys had at last found something which they could understand and appreciate. Many of the beauties of the poem were lost to them, still they understood enough to enjoy it. Martin declared that he could see the stag as it "sniffed the tainted gale," sprung to its feet, shook the dew-drops from its flanks, and bounded off toward the mountains. What would the poet have thought could he have heard the remarks of his two young admirers beyond the ocean? They wondered if the hounds could run faster than Bounce; they wondered why the huntsman did not shoot the deer, little knowing that it was long before the invention of the flint-lock or rifle; they wondered and wondered about many things which their simple and untrained minds could not grasp or understand.

"Why, I almost forgot that news about the cave," said Owen when the two boys were tired of the poem.

"Let me hear it. You don't know how often I think about that place."

"The other night when I was reading 'Robinson Crusoe'—"

"Tell me about the cave. I've had enough about books for one night," interrupted Martin.

"That's just what I'm trying to do."

"Pardon me. I thought you were going to speak of the old man and his island."

"No. While I had the book in my hand I happened to see some writing and drawing on one of the last pages. There was a line marked *Beech Fork;* above this was the word *hill;* then a few scratches over which were written in two places, *big rocks.* Beginning with these two rocks was a single way or entrance which branched off into a number of passages."

"Were the passages marked?"

"Nothing was written over them; but it seemed to me that the lines represented them."

"Probably they did," said Martin. "Get the book and let us look at them."

"That's the bad luck of it, Mart. The page was burned."

"Who burned it?"

"Well, it was my fault. You see the page was loose; I let the book drop, and the draft from the chimney sucked the leaf into the fire."

"What else was written on that leaf?"

"The word *light* was put down in three different places."

"Did the man show us the night we were there three places where the light entered?"

"No, only two; but of course we didn't see everything."

"I do believe it was a drawing of the cave," said Martin. "But the next question is, who drew it. If we only knew that, we could find out the names of the fellows in the place."

"Nearly every person in the State has read that book," replied Owen. "I don't see what good it would do to get the names."

The boys were silent for some time.

The drawing which Owen had seen was the work of Jerry. When the trapper discovered the cave he went to the Tinker's house and offered to show it to him under certain conditions. Some of these conditions were written on the back of the page which had been burned. If Owen could have examined that page for five minutes he would have known the secret of the cave; for, while the few words scribbled there were unintelligible to others, they were sufficiently plain to any one who had visited the spot.

"I have something else to tell you about the cave," said Owen, who was the first to speak. "You know old Bowen came up here the day after the shooting-match to inquire about Charlie; then he wanted to know where we slept the night we went to the cave."

"How does he know anything about the place?"

"That's just what I don't see; but from the way he asked the question I began to think he knew something about it. Father and mother talk about him every night. Father can't understand how it is that old Bowen's corn-crib has burned the last three years—and burned, mind you, just at the beginning of winter, when he had it full of corn."

"And what has that to do with the cave?" asked Martin.

"Nothing, as far as I can see. But father thinks that old Bowen is a rascal; that something will turn up one of these days and surprise everyone."

"If he does find out about the cave," said Martin, "he will charge that fellow who wants to buy it twice as much as it is worth."

"He won't find out from us. That man treated us kindly. We promised not to tell, and we must keep our promise."

"Just what I think about it, Owen! But I wish the fellow would hurry on and buy it. You see, we'll spend a whole day going through it."

"Do you think he will take us in as partners, because we've kept the secret so well?" asked Owen.

"I didn't think of that. We can be the guides to show the people around."

"But we must make him let us in as partners."

"Yes, we'll be guides and partners at the same time."

"I wonder whether he will make much money on it."

"And I wonder whether he will be able to buy it soon."

The boys continued for some time to build castles in the air, and to speak of their interest in the cave as if it were already a reality. Their conversation was interrupted by Bounce, who ran out from the porch to the yard-gate barking furiously. They went to the door, but saw no one. It was a poor runaway slave who had caused the disturbance. He had been whipped most cruelly by his master, old Bowen, and threatened with death; and knowing that this was but the beginning of his sufferings, had resolved to attempt an escape. He was now concealed near the yard-gate, in the branches of a small tree. Later in the night he contrived to attract Mose's notice, who, pitying him in his distress, carried him to one of the hay-lofts.

CHAPTER XVI.

On the Trail
of the Runaway Slave.

EARLY THE NEXT MORNING, when old Bowen discovered that the slave had fled, he called his dogs and started in pursuit. It was easy to follow the trail, as it was still fresh. He urged his horse on as fast as it could go, shouted to the dogs, and cursed the fugitive slave. In his hand he held a long, black-snake whip to administer punishment. His eyes sparkled with cruel expectation. His hand grasped the whip firmly, while on, on he rode. The hounds increased their speed. The trail was growing fresher. They would overtake the wretch soon. The heartless master plunged the spurs into his horse's sides, for the dogs were outdistancing him. They passed the Howard house. No! They suddenly stopped in front of the yard-gate. They dashed on, ran wildly in several directions, and returned to the gate. Here they barked, jumped into the air, and scratched around a small tree. The trail ended here. Old Bowen rode up to the spot almost maddened with fury, for Zachary Howard, he thought, had given shelter and protection to his fugitive slave. What revenge! What revenge would be his! Now had his day of retaliation come! He would drag the slave out from his place of concealment, would scourge him in Howard's presence—scourge him until the ground was covered with blood, and the more he writhed and cried for mercy, the harder the lash would fall. If Howard pleaded for him, his punishment would be prolonged. Oh! revenge, cruel, terrible revenge! He leaped from his horse, and, grasping his whip firmly, started toward the house. Mr. Howard, who had been disturbed by the noise, came out to meet him.

"Zach Howard!" cried the raging master, "show me where my slave is concealed. You can't deny it, you have hid him. But I'll find him, and whip him here while you look on—whip him until there is not a drop of blood left in his body. I'll whip him and show you that he is my slave, not yours! Where is he? Bring him out, Zach! Bring him out!"

"There is no slave of yours around these premises," replied the astonished farmer.

"A lie! My dogs tracked him to that tree in front of your gate! Those dogs never fail, Zach, never fail!"

"If the slave was tracked to that tree, Mr. Bowen, he can certainly be tracked farther."

"No sir!" growled old Bowen. "He stopped right there, was helped down by some one, carried away and hid. I have been in this business too long to be deceived by a little scheme like that."

"Strange that this could have happened without my knowing anything about it," said Mr. Howard.

"Well, it did happen, Howard. It happened last night, the trail shows it plainly—shows that he came to the tree and climbed it. The trail doesn't start any place near the tree, and this shows that the cussed negro was helped by some one."

"And why do you think he climbed the tree?" asked Mr. Howard.

"To throw me off the track. The stupid fool! I saw through the trick at the first glance."

"I think I can explain the whole affair."

"How?"

"Do you see that poplar?"

"Yes."

"Do you notice that large limb reaching out toward the tree which you say the negro climbed?"

"Yes. What of it?"

"Don't you think that the negro could have climbed from the small tree into the large one?"

"Possibly. But what did he do when he got in the large tree?"

"Don't you notice that from the other side of the poplar there is another long branch extending over my carriage-house?"

"Yes! yes!"

"Don't you see plainly that he could have climbed on the roof?"

"Yes! What then?"

"The rest of the work was easy."

"How? how?"

"He let himself down from the eaves to the rail-fence, and then crawled along."

"You've got the whole trail knit together nicely," said old Bowen, deeply wounded and humiliated because he had failed to connect the facts.

"Ha! ha! I'll get him now! And how I'll lash him!" he continued, with satanic glee, at the same time calling his dogs and starting for the fence, where he hoped to find the lost trail.

"But hold! Mr. Bowen, why are you so cruel with your slaves? If you treated them kindly, they wouldn't run away."

"Zach Howard!" cried old Bowen, "those slaves are mine! They are mine, and I'll whip them as often as I wish—whip them just to hear them yell, if I choose to do so. That's my answer to your question."

"And my answer to you is this," retorted Mr. Howard, in a tone of voice that made Louis Bowen quail before him, "you are a heartless wretch, with whom I'll have nothing in common. Never again cross the threshold of my door, or enter this yard. If you do—"

"No threats are necessary," interrupted Bowen. "I hate and despise you too much for that. Now that you have shown me how and where to find my slave, I have no further use for your company." He wheeled around and started off to find the trail.

Mr. Howard regretted that he had given the information. It was too late, however, to amend matters, so he went into the house, and from one of the upper windows, where he could get a full view of the scene, eagerly watched old Bowen in his vain attempts to follow up the trail. After riding up and down either side of the fence for about an hour, the master grew tired of the fruitless labor, and regretted that he had disposed of Mr. Howard's services so quickly. Still, not having the courage to return and ask for help, he spurred his horse on toward the river, where he hoped to find a new clue to the direction taken by the runaway.

The escaped slave, trembling with fright, watched the whole proceedings from a crevice in the hayloft, and when his master had disappeared he sank back upon the hay exhausted. For days and weeks he suffered from his sore and emaciated back. The negro, Mose, came to him regularly three times a day, bringing him food and applying salve to his wounds.

When asked why he had been whipped, the poor slave would only answer: "He'll kill me if I tell; he'll kill me if I tell." After a month had passed, the wounds were entirely healed, and Mose suggested to his friend that he should start out again and try to make his escape to some more northern State. But the poor wretch was afraid to leave his place of concealment, knowing that if he were caught, a worse punishment, even death, would be his fate.

CHAPTER XVII.

Carrying the News.

IT WAS the morning of the twenty-fifth of January, 1815. Martin Cooper rode up before Mr. Howard's and, dismounting, called Owen, whom he saw busy with the chores around the house.

"Owen," said he, "look at this! Father was working at the barn yesterday, and found it in the saddle pockets— it's one of the prize pistols you won at the shooting-match. I don't know how it got into the pockets. Why didn't you speak about it?"

"Why, Martin!" was the answer, "I thought you would find it as soon as you got home. I slipped it into the pockets just before we parted."

"I've brought it back, Owen. You mustn't give it to me."

"Keep it, Mart! You did as much to get the pistols as I. When I told them here at home that I had given you one of the prizes, they all said you deserved it."

"No, Owen! it wouldn't be right for me to take your prize."

"Right, nothing. It's yours, Mart, and you have got to keep it."

"I can't."

"You must," and with playful firmness Owen quickly replaced the pistol in the saddle pockets, and secured the buckles.

"But look!" he continued, running toward the gate, "there comes a man with a flag."

"Hurrah, boys!" cried the stranger, riding up at full speed. "Hurrah! Our soldiers have whipped the English in a great battle at New Orleans. Not more than a dozen of our men killed. Two thousand of the red-coats have been captured, killed or wounded. Here is the account of the battle written by Jackson; and this is the flag carried by the Kentucky regiment."

"Hurrah! hurrah!" chimed in the two boys, throwing their caps into the air. "Hurrah for the American soldiers! Hurrah for the Kentuckians!"

Mr. Howard heard the shouting, and came out into the yard. He was overjoyed at the report, and taking the bullet-rent flag he waved it three times over his head, invoking a blessing on his country.

"We have no time to lose," said the stranger. "This flag and this report must be carried to Washington. The man who handed it to me on the banks of the Green river killed his horse, he rode so fast. I have been on the road since four this morning, and my horse can not go a mile farther. Someone here must take my place."

Owen and Martin interchanged a rapid glance, and demanded at the same time the privilege of heralding the victory.

"Go, my boys! It is no small honor to carry such a flag and such news, and both of you shall have it," said Mr. Howard. "Owen, hurry on and saddle Hickory. Martin, leave your saddle pockets here, but take out the pistol which you and Owen were speaking of. It is yours; buckle it around your waist. It will look more like war. And now, stranger," he continued, turning to the man, "you are welcome! Walk into the house. I'll have breakfast ready for you in a short time, and we'll see that one of the negroes takes care of your horse."

"Before the boys start," said the stranger, "I must say a word to them about giving the flag, and especially the message, to a reliable person. They were entrusted to an officer of one of our Kentucky regiments. He changed horses eight times before he reached Tennessee. The last horse dropped in a marshy country, and the poor fellow was forced to push his way on foot for five miles before he came to a settlement. He fell exhausted at the door of a farmer's house. The message has been given to four persons since that time. If the boys can carry it to Louisville, the soldiers there will see it safe to Pittsburg; beyond that the forts are so close that it can be carried one hundred and fifty miles in twenty-four hours."

"I can easily arrange the matter," replied Mr. Howard; "there is a friend of mine by the name of Sims, who lives twelve miles beyond Bardstown on the Louisville road; he is a true patriot in whose hands the letter will be safe. The boys can carry the message twenty miles, and friend Sims can take it twenty-eight more."

Martin and Owen were soon ready for their long ride, strapping their pistols around their waists and hanging their powder flasks at their sides.

"This flag for you," said the stranger, handing it to Martin; "and this for you," he continued, giving Jackson's letter to Owen. "Give it to no one except your father's friend. The President, Congress, and the whole country are waiting anxiously for the news from New Orleans; but I have my reasons for suspecting that there are some unprincipled wretches who would gladly intercept such joyful tidings. Even if you die for it, my boy, do not give this letter to any one but the man who is to carry it to Louisville."

Owen's heart beat with patriotic pride as he placed the missive deep down in his coat pocket, and promised to guard it faithfully.

The whole family came out to bid the boys "God speed." When Martin waved the flag, and both he and Owen fired a farewell salute from their pistols, they were answered by shouts while hats and bonnets were tossed in the air. Little Robin, who, as the reader has seen, was always frightened at the report of a fire-arm, sought shelter behind Mrs. Howard's apron; while Wash, who thought that Owen never fired a pistol without killing something, sallied forth in quest of the victim.

My readers have all heard of "Paul Revere's Ride," and how the patriot, spreading the news from farm to farm, aroused the American yeomen to battle with the British regulars.

> *"How the farmers gave them ball for ball,*
> *From behind each fence and farm-yard wall,*
> *Chasing the red-coats down the lane,*
> *Then crossing the fields to emerge again,*
> *Under the trees at the turn of the road,*
> *And only pausing to fire and load."*

The tidings which our young friends carried resembled in some respects the message of Paul Revere—his was the cry of battle, theirs the shout of victory; he called his countrymen to defend their rights, they proclaimed that their country's wrongs had been redressed. On they sped, their young hearts burning with patriotic pride. Firing their pistols to attract the attention of the farmers near the road, pausing for a moment to show the flag and tell the good news, then dashing on again, in less than two hours the boys were galloping up the hill in sight of Bardstown.

They remembered, however, that it was county court day, and that the town would be filled with visitors. They therefore determined upon a definite course of action. Martin, according to the arrangement, was to ride into the midst of the crowd, show the flag and announce the victory. Owen, on his part, was to remain at one side, and if the written report of the battle were demanded, to put spurs to his horse and escape from the town; for they were determined to be true to their charge, and under no conditions to surrender the message to another for a single instant.

The public square, as it was called, a large open lot in the middle of the town, was crowded with townfolk and farmers from all parts of the county. These were engaged in a variety of ways—some entered the stone court house to follow the proceedings of the bar, while others stood around in groups chatting about their crops, and inquiring about the latest reports of the war. But by far the greater number was engaged in trading horses and cattle, or purchasing various articles of the peddlers who came to town in great numbers on court days.

Suddenly the attention of all was attracted in the same direction, for Martin and Owen rode into the public square, checking their horses in the midst of the crowd and crying out: "Hurrah for the Americans! The English army has been defeated at New Orleans!" As Martin preceded Owen, and carried the flag, the eyes of all were directed toward him.

A wild shout of triumph answered the announcement of the victory. Then the crowd pressed around and demanded the particulars of the battle.

"Who brought the news from the South?"

"When was the battle fought?"

"How many were killed?"

"Where did that flag come from?"

"Are you sure about the result?"

"Have you any written account of the battle?"

Such were the questions which came from every side, but the shouts and hurrahs were so prolonged and loud that Martin was no longer heard. A few men who were nearest to him demanded the written account of the battle. Martin replied that he had orders not to show it to any one. The men became excited at once, and threatened to drag him from his horse. The boy saw that he was powerless; turning therefore toward Owen, who was ready to start at a moment's notice, he signaled to him to go. Owen understood the sign, sank his spurs into old Hickory's side, and dashed down the road toward Louisville.

At the same time Martin was dragged from his horse by several strong men and forced by them through the crowd into the court house. Here he easily succeeded in explaining his conduct, and why it was that his companion had escaped with Jackson's message. The county judge learned from him the full account of the battle, as contained in the written report of the commander; then going out upon the steps of the court house repeated the news to the excited throng. The town was wild with enthusiasm! An old cannon, which years before had been used to defend Bardstown when it was a frontier post, was dragged out into the street and was made once more to raise its thundering voice. Old heroes of the Revolution were there—old soldiers who had fought at Trenton and Yorktown. Some of these who had treasured up their rust-worn muskets marched in line and fired salutes.

At the west end of the town, workmen were busily engaged on the new cathedral; its steeple was already completed, and in it hung a bell, whose mellowed notes had never yet been heard in the western hemisphere. This bell was four feet in height and eight in circumference, and was destined for years to be the largest in the country from the Allegheny Mountains to the Pacific Ocean. For more than a century it had hung in an old Gothic steeple, in the northern part of Europe, and called pious pilgrims and holy monks to prayer and meditation. When impious hands destroyed the sacred shrine, the bell was spared and transported beyond the seas, where, wreathed with evergreens, it waited the day when it would again give forth its harmonious notes.

Near the church stood the saintly, zealous Bishop Flaget, contemplating the work before him. His meditation was disturbed by the shouts of victory; then came the report that it was in honor of the American success at the battle of New Orleans. At once he caught the enthusiasm of those around; raising his voice he cried aloud to the workmen in the steeple: "Ring the bell! Ring the bell! The American army has been victorious at New Orleans!" Long and loud it rang mingling its mellow notes with the roar of the cannon and announcing peace to all.

CHAPTER XVIII.

Saving the Message.

When Owen had gone some distance from the town, and realized that he was not pursued, he stopped for a few minutes, hoping that Martin would extricate himself from the crowd and overtake him. As he glanced down the road over which he had passed, he descried two horsemen galloping toward him; suspecting the object of their mission, he prepared for a second flight at the least sign of danger. When the two men were within a hundred yards of him, one checked his horse, while the other continued to gallop straight ahead. Not wishing to be surprised, Owen started out at a brisk gait. "Stop there, young fellow! they want to see that message at the court-house!" cried out the man who was nearest to him.

"Go it, Hickory! go it, old fellow!" was Owen's only reply; at the same time he plied the spurs vigorously.

"Stop there! I tell you, stop there!" again cried the man, laying the whip to his horse's side and following in hot pursuit.

Owen glanced behind—the man was gaining on him.

The boy leaned far over on the horse's neck, stroked his mane and said: "Go on, Hickory! don't let him catch us, go on! go on!"

"Say! youngster! If you don't stop there, I'll thrash you when I catch you!" cried the angered pursuer.

"But you won't catch me," thought Owen, for Hickory was now gaining a little, and his young rider knew that he was no mean runner.

The man was evidently not prepared for a long race; he beat his horse cruelly, urging the poor animal on at its utmost speed. Again Owen looked behind—again the man was gaining on him.

He saw that his pursuer was making one mighty effort to overtake him; he plunged his spur deep into the side of his faithful beast. The enraged animal sprang forward: The race was nearly even for a full quarter of a mile. Now Owen gained, and now the angry man behind. Hickory slipped and nearly fell in the soft, muddy road. The man yelled in triumph, gaining twenty yards in a few minutes. Then Hickory was on again—Owen slowly recovered lost ground. The man shouted to frighten him—this, however, had the effect of making him goad his horse the more. He saw the man gradually drop behind, and then abandon the unequal race. Owen pushed on briskly for about a mile, when he too paused to give the horse a much needed rest.

Eight miles of the road still remained to be traveled, and as Owen now felt secure he proceeded slowly, occasionally looking behind to see whether or not the man would continue the pursuit. He had gone about another mile, when to his astonishment the man reappeared riding another horse. Could Hickory stand the race for seven miles? Owen doubted, yet he resolved to save the message or kill the horse. The man on his part regarded the result as only a matter of time, for his horse was fresh, and would sooner or later overtake the wearied animal which he followed.

On went the boy, on came the man. On, on they rode, past the farm houses by the wayside, past the fallow fields and leafless woods which seemed to take wings and fly behind. On, on they sped, now darting down some rough, steep hill, now clambering up the rocky ascent on the opposite side. A settler, cutting wood close to the road, heard the clatter of hoofs, and, dropping his axe, watched with bated breath the onward rush of the boy and man. Little did he dream that the boy was carrying a message of victory and peace; that the man was a veritable Arnold in the hatred of his country. Yet the settler's sympathies were with the boy. He admired, too, the youth's superior horsemanship. How gallantly he bestrode his horse! "Go it, my lad, go it!" he shouted. "You're a fine rider, and I reckon you'll win." On, on they plunged, the boy and man, and the settler was far behind. Another farm house was reached. In front of it a country urchin was swinging on a gate. He climbed to the top of the gate-post to view the race, laughed with delight as he saw the sparks struck from the stony road, and waved his ragged hat in boisterous glee. Past him they fled. A few minutes later, and the urchin was far behind.

But soon old Hickory began to lag. Yard by yard the man drew closer to the boy. Owen saw plainly that the race was over.

"Back! stop there!" cried he, at the same time drawing his pistol. But the man came on.

"Stop! stop there! or I'll wound your horse," said the boy, pointing the pistol toward the advancing enemy.

The man, however, seemed to realize the difficulty of firing with any accuracy under such conditions; he, therefore, lowered his head behind the horse's neck to escape any stray ball, and continued to ride on. Owen was true to his threat, and taking deliberate aim, he sent a ball through one of the animal's front legs; the horse fell to the ground unable to arise.

Still the pursuit did not end here, for old Hickory began to stagger and reel from one side of the road to the other.

"Poor old Hickory! poor old fellow!" said Owen, stroking the animal's neck and mane.

Hickory turned his head as if to beseech his young master not to urge him farther.

"Poor old fellow!" continued Owen, trying in vain to keep back the tears that gathered in his eyes; for Hickory was a true friend of his, and it pained the boy to make him suffer so.

Hickory stopped—he could go no farther!

Owen dug the spurs deep into his side, crying at the same time: "Poor! poor old Hickory! I have to do it; can't you go? Can't you go, old Hickory?"

The jaded beast made another effort, trembled in every limb, and fell heavily to the ground. The man whose horse had been shot gave a yell and started on a run toward Owen, who quickly extricated himself from the stirrups and ran down the road.

"I'll give you a sound thrashing when I catch you!" cried the man, as both pursuer and pursued rushed along over the rough road. "You see I am gaining on you!" he continued, after a few minutes, "you may as well give up."

Owen didn't think so; at least it was evident from the way he ran that he intended to continue the race as long as he was able to move.

"Say, youngster," resumed the man, "the Salt river is about a quarter of a mile ahead; I'll get you when we come to it."

Owen did not answer, but continued straight on.

"If you stop now I won't whip you," shouted the man.

But his threats and promises were equally fruitless.

"And if you don't stop I'll go back and kill your horse after I have taken your letter from you!"

Owen felt this keenly, yet he remembered the promise he had made before he left his father's house, and for no consideration would he be unfaithful to it. The man continued to yell, to promise, to threaten, while both continued to run; not very fast, it is true, for the man had decided for himself that Owen would be forced to surrender on the bank of the Salt river, which was at no great distance away.

Soon the dreaded river appeared, covered with floating ice. All hope seemed to be lost! The very thought of jumping into the icy stream sent a shudder through the frame of the exhausted boy! The man now began to run at full speed, for he feared that Owen would dart off into the woods. The bank was reached! No time was left for deliberation! The man was only twenty yards away!

"You shall not have it!" cried Owen, facing his pursuer and shaking the letter above his head. With these words he rushed into the water among the cakes of floating ice. As this was a ford and the usual place for crossing, the river was not deep. But the current was swift, and it seemed at any moment that it would sweep him away.

Bravely our little hero pushed his way through the battering ice, while the angry man on the shore cursed him, called him a fool, and swore that he would drown if he did not turn back. If ever Owen prayed fervently it was while he battled with that current and ice; he felt that he should be unable to hold his footing if the current became stronger or deeper. He realized, too, that he was weakening fast—the river seemed an angry whirlpool, rushing round and round and carrying him in its cold and frothy eddy. How chilled he was! His teeth chattered and his whole body trembled! Could he reach the opposite shore? It was not ten feet away! Slowly! slowly! still he reached it—thank God, he was safe!

Yet not safe! for unless he find shelter soon he must surely die of cold. On the top of the hill in front of him stood a large frame house. After ten minutes of intense suffering Owen knocked at the door, and, without waiting for an answer, rushed in. Before him sat an elderly man enjoying his after-dinner smoke, in a bright, warm room. It was Mr. Sims. Owen had accomplished his mission—the letter was safe.

Mr. Sims naturally supposed that Owen had fallen from his horse while attempting to ford the river. He saw that the boy was extremely weak, and ordered him to bed at once. Owen told his story briefly, and handed the official document to the farmer. Before the sun had set, it was placed in the hands of the commanding officer at the little fort near the falls of the Ohio. From Louisville to Pittsburg, from Pittsburg to Washington—at last the message of General Jackson was delivered to the President.

When the man who had followed Owen for nearly eight miles saw that he was foiled in his attempt, he hastily retraced his steps to the place where he had abandoned his wounded horse. Here he was joined by Tom the Tinker, who had set out with him from Bardstown, but lagged behind, since he did not wish to be recognized by Owen.

"The rascal of a boy shot this horse just as I was about to overtake him," said the man, as the Tinker came up to him.

"The message—did you get the message?"

"How could I when he shot the horse?"

"My! my!" continued Tom, in tones of despair, "a hundred dollars for the horse! did not get the message! My! my! And all my work for nothing!"

"And I want the fifty dollars you promised me," interrupted the man.

"You do?"

"Yes, I do! Did I not ride my horse half to death before you borrowed that second one from the farmer?"

"But you didn't get the message."

"I am going to have that money. I worked hard enough for it. I followed the little devil until—until he jumped into the river."

"And where was his horse?" asked Tom.

"It gave out, too. There it is up there," answered the man, pointing to the place where old Hickory was lying, apparently dead.

"Perhaps the boy was drowned while trying to cross the river," said the Tinker.

"I watched him until he came to Sims'."

"Then he's safe."

"Of course he is. At least, you'll never see that message. I won't be surprised, however, if the boy dies."

"I hope he does," said Tom. "Those Howards have been in my way for fifteen years. You see, they live near me. I hate every one of them!"

"See here! I want my fifty dollars," interrupted the man. "I don't care about your Howards and your neighbors. I want my money."

"I promised you fifty dollars if you caught the boy. I'll give you ten for your work."

"Not a cent less than fifty," demanded the man.

"Say twenty-five and you shall have it," replied Tom.

"If you don't give me fifty dollars we are going to fight here!" growled the angry man, at the same time grasping the reins of the Tinker's horse.

As much as Tom the Tinker loved his money, he was not willing to fight for it; he therefore gave the man the full amount. Then he paid a hundred dollars more for the horse which he had borrowed from his accomplice, and which Owen had shot. He then rode off toward Bardstown, uttering imprecations against the boy who had thwarted him, against the man who had robbed him, against everybody and everything. How was he to regain the money which he had lost? For a long time he sought an answer to this question. He seemed to have solved the difficulty before he reached the town, for he was in the best of spirits. Here he consulted several men on some secret business, and then proceeded at once to the cave on the banks of the Beech Fork.

Late that same evening Martin joined Owen at Mr. Sims'.

"Did you see old Hickory?" inquired Owen, sitting up in the bed where he had been sleeping.

"Yes!"

"How is he? Tell me quick! How is the poor old fellow?"

"First tell me about yourself, and then we'll see about the horse!"

"Nothing the matter with me. I never felt better, although that was a pretty cold bath I took—and now about Hickory."

"Well, Owen, if you must know it," said Martin, in a broken voice, "the old fellow is dead—stiff—shot through the head."

Owen did not answer, but fell back in the bed and wept bitterly.

When he returned home two days later, what was his surprise to find old Hickory eating away contentedly in his stall. It was the horse wounded by Owen that Martin had seen lying in the road, and in the dark had mistaken for Hickory. As it was impossible for the animal to recover, the owner had shot it through the head.

CHAPTER XIX.

The Tinker Disturbs the Inmates of the Cave.

IT WAS after midnight when Tom the Tinker reached the cave.

"Have you heard the news?" he inquired of Stayford, who seemed to be the only occupant of the dingy abode.

"News! What news?" growled Stayford. "We hear nothing in this hole. Jerry and myself spend our whole time working for you. I am tired of it, Tom, and it's got to stop. That's the news I've for you!"

"Don't be hard on me, Stayford," said the Tinker in almost piteous tones. "I've lost a hundred and fifty dollars to-day. My! my! a hundred and fifty dollars!"

"And is this the news you wished to give me?" demanded Stayford.

"No; it was this. Our troops have whipped the English at New Orleans. The war is over, and there will be no more tax on whisky."

"And then all of our work will be for nothing?"

"It seems so, Stayford; it seems so. But where is Jerry? I've business news to communicate to both of you."

"He just went to bed. Since you weren't here to help him, he had to work hard for fully fifteen hours to keep the mash from souring." Stayford now spoke in the most friendly way. At the approach of danger he forgot that he was angry.

"Let him sleep!" said the Tinker, as he and Stayford seated themselves on a pile of wood at the end of the cave. "We can settle the affair; he will agree to it, I know he will. First, let me tell you about the hundred and fifty dollars. I wanted to take revenge on those men at Washington for putting me in prison and robbing me when I was in the whisky business in Pennsylvania twenty years ago. Every man, from the President down to the lowest officer, had a hand in the work. They ruined me when I was a rich man; for years and years I've been waiting to square up accounts with them. I had a chance to-day, but it failed. I was going to change Jackson's letter, and put the English down as the winners. This would have frightened the authorities at Washington, and they wouldn't find out their mistake for a month. It is probable that the whisky tax would have been doubled."

"And why didn't you get the general's message about the battle?" interrupted Stayford.

"Ah! Stayford, it is all your fault! If you had killed that young Howard last fall when I had him in this cave we should be rich men to-day. He carried the message from his father's house to old Sims' farm. I offered a man fifty dollars—fifty dollars; just think of it!—if he secured it. The man's horse gave out. I hired another— young Howard shot it. Then young Howard's horse fell and could go no farther. He left it, waded across an ice-cold river and saved the letter. There's the whole story for you—money gone, whisky gone—all gone, because we spared the life of a Howard!"

Tom was angry—very angry. He rose from his seat and paced the floor of the cave, muttering his broken sentences. Stayford grew angry, too, for it seemed that Tom was shifting the whole failure on him, since he had saved Martin and Owen the night they entered the cave. However, he overlooked the slight, as he wished to learn whether Tom had heard anything definite about the battle. The Americans had gained a decided victory! This was all the Tinker knew about it.

"And the war is over?" said Stayford.

"Yes, and the hundreds of barrels of whisky which we have been storing away in this cave are a dead loss if we can't sell them in six months. I sold thirty barrels to-day at twenty cents below tax."

"What's that?"

"Thirty barrels to-day, before I left Bardstown. We get ten cents extra on each gallon; it isn't much, but it's better than keeping the whisky until you can't give it away."

"When and how is it to be delivered?"

"Six barrels to-morrow. We'll pay Simpson well and get him off before sunrise."

Stayford was astounded at the Tinker's boldness. For three years they had worked at their trade only at night, and had guarded their movements with the utmost secrecy. And now to go to the other extreme and deliver whisky in open daylight seemed little short of insanity.

When Jerry heard of the scheme the wary old trapper shook his head and remarked: "That's usin' new kinds of dead-falls to ketch foxes. I reckon Stayford and me can stan' it if you can, Tom. If we're caught in our own traps we can stay hare in the den and fight a whole pack of hounds."

Simpson, a workman, who had lately joined the other three men in the cave, agreed to deliver the whisky, and was to receive extra payment for each load. A little before sunrise he had the team ready. An old oaken beam which served the double purpose of door and a means of loading was lowered—the barrels were let down into the wagon and carefully covered with straw. Everything had been so arranged that neither the horses, the wagon, nor the whisky could be identified, even if taken by the town authorities.

It was about ten o'clock when he reached the town. Passing along one of the principal streets, toward an old stable, where the barrels were to be delivered, Simpson was congratulating himself on his success, when he chanced to turn and see a little boy sitting on the wagon-bed.

"Get down, there!" he stammered.

Whereat the urchin dropped off into the mud, making wry faces at the driver and yelling: "Corn juice! Corn juice!"

"Shut up! you rascal!" cried Simpson, rising from his seat and feigning to pursue him with his blacksnake whip. The boy made good his retreat, leaving Simpson to proceed without further molestation. After unloading the barrels, he remained in town for an hour to give his horses a rest and then started for home.

He had gone about a mile, when he was startled by the sound of voices and the clatter of hoofs. Was he pursued? Yes; three men were after him, well armed and mounted. The long blacksnake lashed the horses, they ran as they had never run before; the heavy wain rattled over the rough road, bounding over boulders, falling into ruts, throwing streams of muddy water from all four wheels. The wagon-bed was loosened and rolled off. Simpson took refuge on the front axle, and used the whip still more freely. The horsemen gained on him, however, yelling as they advanced. Following the next impulse of self-preservation, he leaped from the wagon, clambered up the steep hillside, and, running through the woods for half a mile, concealed himself in a hollow tree.

The men who were pursuing him—or rather who had frightened him, for they were not in pursuit—overtook the team and tied it at the side of the road, thinking that the owner would return and get it on discovering his mistake. They had been in town for the night's celebration, and on their return were just sober enough to realize that the teamster was trying to escape from them. This induced them to follow him, and the faster he ran the more they enjoyed the joke. That same afternoon some pilfering travelers passing along the road and seeing the wagon without an owner, boldly loaded it with their own luggage and drove on.

Simpson remained in the hollow tree until night, and then made his way toward the cave. When within two hundred yards of it he saw the dark outline of some one standing in the narrow footpath directly in front of him. At once he darted off into the thick underbrush.

"Simpson! Simpson! Is that you, Simpson?" called out a voice.

It was the Tinker. Simpson retraced his steps.

"The wagon!" demanded Tom.

"Captured!"

"The team!"

"Gone!"

"The whisky!"

"Gone, too!"

"Speak out, Simpson! tell me! what has happened?"

"All gone! But wait until I get something to eat; besides, you may be arrested if you remain here!"

"Do they know?—Did you tell them?—Do they know my name?" inquired Tom, walking rapidly toward the cave.

"I can't tell you everything at once!" growled Simpson.

"My! my! my! I am ruined! I see it now! I was a fool! My! my! my!"

"What's the matter, old feller?" asked Jerry, as the Tinker entered, followed by the workman, who secured the rock door behind him.

"My! my! my! My money, my money!" continued Tom, throwing himself on a pile of straw and weeping like a child.

When Simpson had satisfied his appetite, he narrated his day's experience.

"Ha! ha! ha!" ejaculated Tom, when he heard that the whisky was safely delivered.

"My! my! my!" he groaned, upon being told that the team was lost.

"What horses did you take?" he anxiously inquired.

"Those you told me to take—Blind and Ruble."

"Nobody knows them; nobody knows them! And what wagon?"

"The one from under the shed."

"Nobody will think it belongs to me!" Tom pronounced these words with evident satisfaction.

"But," he continued, after a short interval, "they cost money! Wagons cost money! Horses cost money! Blind horses cost money! Working day and night—"

"Stop your whimperin', Tom," interrupted Jerry. "It's gone—let it go. We won't be caught in no more traps—won't give the dogs no more fresh trails, and I reckon it'll be all correct in the end."

"It is well enough to say let it go," replied Tom. "You and Stayford lost nothing. You've got nothing to lose. I found you starving dogs when I came here, and—"

"You've kept us starving dogs!" cried Stayford, with a burst of mingled wrath and defiance, at the same time clenching his fist and starting toward the cringing wretch. "Yes, you have kept us starving dogs! We did the work—you got the money. I would like to see you robbed of every cent, put in jail, and then—then hanged!"

"Hare! hare!" interposed Jerry, who had frequently to separate the two, "it's a sorry thing to have the dogs 'round the den; but when the foxes fight inside, it's a darn sight worse."

When peace had been restored, Tom and Simpson left the cave, while Joe and Jerry lay down to take their short repose.

Weeks passed by, and no further signs of discovery were brought to light. The two men within the cave did not leave their safe retreat. Tom did not make his nightly visits. The whisky still and treadmill were idle. One morning Jerry rose from a heavy slumber, and after a short deliberation shook his sleeping companion and said:

"I reckon I have it. If the dogs is on the trail, thare'll be some letters sent to old Squire Grundy down below. The stage passes in a few days. We'll cut her off and take the mail. How's that? Ha!"

"Good enough," replied Stayford. "But while we are waiting I am going out to see how the world looks."

"You had better stay hare until you are sure thar's no danger—no dogs on the trail."

"I can't wait any longer, Jerry. This place is worse than a jail. I am going to find out what has happened."

"Kinder strange way of doin'," said Jerry. "I've heard of many a fox hunt, but never heard of foxes lookin' for dogs."

"I'll never be cornered, you can depend on that. I'll try it alone to-day, and if I cannot learn whether we are suspected, then we'll capture the mail."

CHAPTER XX.

A Day's Sport
Along the Beech Fork.

Patter, patter, let it pour,
Patter, patter, let it roar;
O'er the housetop let it gush,
Down the hillside let it rush.
'Tis a welcome April shower,
And 'twill wake the sweet May flower.

THUS MUSED OWEN as he sat late one afternoon husking corn, while the pelting rain overhead recalled some old nursery rhymes which he had learned by heart when a mere child. "No, it isn't April yet, and it will be a long time before we have May flowers. It's about the middle of March; I reckon the black-perch ought to bite now. It will be too wet to plow this week; so I'll ask father to let Martin and me go a-fishing." And he worked hard at his task to have the corn shelled before dark.

"Why, father, it's time to fish for black-perch," said he to Mr. Howard, who appeared at the door of the corn crib.

"I reckon it's time for you to have that corn ready for the mill," replied the farmer.

"I'll finish it to-day, take it to the mill to-morrow— and then may Martin and I go fishing on Thursday?" asked Owen.

"What about that field along the river to be plowed?" inquired the farmer. "You are getting to be a big boy now, and must be prepared to do your share of the work on the farm."

"Plow after this heavy rain?"

"Yes, when it is dry enough."

"But it won't be dry this week," argued Owen.

"Well, you may go fishing this week; that is, one day of this week. Then be ready for hard work—no fishing, no hunting for some time."

Mr. Howard was more than willing to let his son enjoy a day along the Beech Fork; still, it was evident from his way of speaking that he intended to keep him busily engaged during the coming month while getting the ground ready for the spring corn.

"Think you can go fishing to-morrow?" asked Owen of Martin on the following day while on his way from the mill.

"I reckon I can. It's too wet to plow, and there's nothing else to be done this time of the year."

"Better find out now."

"Father isn't here. It'll be all right; you can depend on me, and if anything happens to keep me from going I'll ride over and let you know to-night."

"Did you examine those reeds that we cut last fall?" asked Owen.

"No! haven't thought of them since."

"Well, I broke mine, and I'll have to depend on you for one."

"I can easily give you a dozen. We cut at least twenty-four, and half of them belong to you. They're well seasoned, too—been hanging in the barn for six months. I'll bring two along to-morrow, and you can get the others the next time our wagon passes by your house."

The reeds referred to grew in patches along the Beech Fork. The boys generally cut them in the fall to have them dry and seasoned for the spring fishing.

"I must hurry on home and fix the minnow net," said Owen, starting off.

"Good-bye."

"I'll meet you at the creek."

Old Hickory trotted off with Owen and the sack of meal.

Uncle Pius had taught Owen and Martin how to fish for the black-bass (or black-perch, as they are called in that section of the country) when the boys were quite small. Under his direction they had become expert fishermen. They knew nothing of the various contrivances described by Irving in "The Angler," nor were they equipped like our modern fisherman during his summer vacation—rods of split bamboo, patent reels and landing nets would have appeared useless to them.

When first accompanying Uncle Pius on his fishing expeditions they were surprised to find that he caught a perch every time he had a bite, while they lost minnow after minnow.

"Uncle Pius, you've got a bite, you've got a bite!" they would often exclaim, as his red-cedar float disappeared below the water. The old negro, however, seemed to take no notice of their warning. He remained motionless for a few seconds as if lost in deep thought, then gave a quick jerk to fasten the hook, and landed his prize, much to the admiration and astonishment of his young companions. One day the fish were biting rapidly. Uncle Pius had secured a nice string of perch, while Owen and Martin had made their usual record—bite, bite, bite, but not a fish.

"Uncle Pius," said Owen, "I'm getting tired of this. I wish you'd show us how to fish."

"Yes," chimed in Martin, "we've lost a bucketful of minnows and haven't caught one perch."

"Well, Massar Ow'n and Massar Martin," said the grave old negro, laying aside his reed and assuming an air of professional dignity, "dis am an awful good proposishion (he meant occasion) for to larn how to ketch perks, for dey's awful hungry to-day and is bitin' right smart—some days dey bite right scattarin'.

I would hab tole you long 'fore dis how to fish, but I know'd you'd say dat you know'd all about fishin' before this old niggar told you. Fust, you must know how to put the minnar on de hook," he continued, taking a large shiner from the bucket and baiting the hook with great care. "Run de hook right fru de lower lip—see dar; den right fru the upper lip—see dar, just a little 'low de eye—see dar; not too deep, or you'll kill the critter—see dar."

Uncle Pius handed the pole to Owen, told him to cast out near a fallen tree, and not to pull until the perch started off with the line. Owen had not to wait long for a bite. His float soon disappeared, and although Uncle Pius yelled "let 'im go, chile," the young fisherman in his excitement jerked with all his force, missed the fish, and entangled his line among the branches overhead.

"You's always a-rushin'," expostulated the old negro.

While Owen climbed the tree to get the line, Martin took his lesson in fishing, and was determined not to pull until Uncle Pius gave the signal.

"How do you know when to pull?" he asked.

"Dar ain't no rule, Massar Martin; it kindar comes natu'al when one knows how."

Soon the cedar float went under. It was evident from the rapidity with which it disappeared that no small perch had bitten. The few brief seconds that followed seemed an hour. Martin trembled with excitement; still he waited for the word to pull.

"Dar's de time!" cried out Uncle Pius, as he saw the line stretch.

"I've got it, and a big one!" yelled Martin in triumph.

"Up here with it," shouted Owen from among the branches overhead.

"Keep the line a-stretchin'!" exclaimed Uncle Pius, "or he's a gonnar."

He had scarcely uttered these words when the fish leaped into the air, shook the hook from its mouth, and disappeared into the water.

"Jes' as I'se sayin'," remarked the old negro. "Now, Massar Martin, you've larned how to ketch perks, and you must larn how to lan' 'em."

"Is there anything to be learned about landing a perch?" inquired Martin, with surprise. "When you catch a catfish there is no danger of its getting off; in fact, you remember that we cut the heads off of several to get out the hooks."

"Dar's an awful 'stonishin' dif'erens 'tween a catfish and a perk," interposed Uncle Pius. "It's hard to keep a perk on, an' it's hard to get a catfish off. If ebbar you let de line slack de perk'll shake de hook from his mouth in free shakes of a sheep's tail."

"Here it goes again," said Martin. "I'll not only catch the first perch that bites, but will land it in a tip-top way."

From his position among the overhanging branches Owen watched Martin's next attempt with interest, while Uncle Pius, conscious of the dignity of his position, gravely directed the movements of his young disciple.

"Nebbar stop," said he. "Jest keep a-pullin' when you got him. Keep a-pullin' slow, an' you'll fetch him, sure's de rain helps young corn."

Martin followed directions carefully, and succeeded in landing the next perch.

"Hurrah!" he yelled in triumph, "that's a fine one, and here goes for another."

Before Owen had time to climb down the tree and bait his hook Martin had secured perch number two.

The two boys went to work in earnest, and, although many a perch escaped from them, in less than an hour they had fully a dozen fish on their string. Uncle Pius watched their progress with evident satisfaction, now yelling to Martin "to keep de line a-pullin'," and to Owen "not to be a-rushin'."

"Massar Martin and Massar Owen," he said to the boys when it was time to go, "you know how to fish for perks, but don't forget dat dis ole niggar larned you."

The first lesson of Uncle Pius was given some two years before our story commenced. On the morning to which we referred in this chapter our two young friends started out, not as tyros, but as experienced fishers.

On reaching the river the boys selected a spot near a fallen sycamore, where the water was about four feet deep, and the bank around was rocky and clear from all underbrush. This would enable them to land the perch without fear of tangling their lines.

On the way to the river, however, they did not notice that a man was following them for more than a mile through the forest, at times close enough to overhear their conversation without any risk of being discovered by them. It was Walter Stayford. He was evidently dogging their footsteps with a purpose. The ground over which he passed was certainly known to him, for even when he lost sight of the boys he followed them as a hound follows a fresh trail.

When the boys came to the river he ensconced himself behind a fallen log, where he could hear every word they uttered. What could be his object in watching them so closely? He certainly did not seek their lives, for he had many a chance to kill them in the depth of the forest. Besides, was not he the man who befriended them during that eventful night in the cave? Had they not shown their gratitude by keeping the secret which they had promised so faithfully to keep? That the cave had been discovered was not their fault. Tom the Tinker—he alone was answerable for this! And at the very thought of the old miser Stayford's face flushed with anger. With difficulty he stifled the curse he was about to utter, as he lay there listening to the boys.

"Now for good luck," said Martin, as he threw his minnow near the branches of the fallen tree.

"And here goes for a three-pounder," chimed in Owen, dropping his minnow on the opposite side of the sycamore.

Five minutes passed. The boys played their minnows up and down the stream, threw them out and pulled them in, vainly hoping to attract a fish.

"No three-pounder yet," said Owen, who, as the reader has seen, had not the patience of his companion.

"No, not yet," replied Martin, still manoeuvering with his line. "Not yet, but they'll come soon. We can't expect the perch to be waiting at the exact spot where we chance to stop."

"And they can't expect us to wait all day for them," rejoined Owen, with a laugh.

"Give them a fair trial—say fifteen minutes more."

"All right," and Owen took out his father's watch, which he had borrowed for the day.

"Look at your bobber!" cried Martin before two minutes had passed.

"Where?"

"It's gone! Pull!"

Owen did pull, but it was too late, for he had lost his minnow.

"That wasn't a perch," said he. "Surely it wasn't a turtle, for they don't bite until warm weather."

"Surely it was a turtle," said Martin. "There it is."

As he spoke a large mossback came to the surface, and calmly surveyed the surroundings, as if to say: "Well, my little boy, that's all you know about turtles biting before warm weather."

"There's a target for us," said Martin. "Let him have a bullet."

As quick as a flash both boys grasped their pistols, which they took pride in wearing whenever they went into the woods or along the river, and fired at the same instant. One ball pierced the turtle's head. It gave several clumsy strokes, then gradually sunk, leaving a bloody streak behind.

From his place of concealment Stayford watched this exhibition of skill. "It's well for me that I'm not here to meet those boys in a fair fight with pistols," he thought to himself. "How quick it was done, too. Of course it was that young Owen. He seems to handle a pistol as well as he does a rifle, and the very pistol he won at the shooting-match. How I would like to have one of that make," and Walter Stayford examined the rusty cap and ball revolver which hung at his side.

"Your bullet hit him," said Owen, who thought that in his eagerness to fire rapidly he had shot above the turtle.

"I reckon it's hard to judge," replied Martin.

"I reckon not!" muttered Stayford to himself, for in his opinion only the youthful victor of the shooting-match could have performed such a feat.

"No; I aimed too high," said Owen in response to Martin's doubt.

"That's bad luck, at any rate," Martin grumbled, "we've lost the turtle and frightened away the perch."

"I am willing to give them the full fifteen minutes; they have—have eight minutes left," replied Owen.

"In goes the minnow—and under goes the bobber—

and out comes the first—first—first perch!" cried Martin, with excitement, at the same time landing a perch weighing about a pound.

"That must be a straggler," said Owen, "let's see whether he brought a companion along."

He threw in his line at the same place, and almost the same moment, as his float moved slowly off, began to repeat, "I—I—I—have—have—have—ve—a fine one," and when he finished the last word he pulled in a perch twice the size of Martin's.

"Good!" shouted Martin; "I wonder what brought him around."

"Don't know; but now for the fun if we have struck a school of them."

For four hours the boys did not move from the spot. Fish after fish was landed, until a string of forty perch was the reward of their day's effort.

"Only six minnows left," at last said Owen, feeling in the bucket for another bait.

"Wait a moment," interposed Martin, "let's try the new way. An old fisherman told me the other day that he always baited the shiners through the back, because in this position they appeared more natural."

"Now's a good time to try," said Owen, "for we can afford to lose a few minnows. How did he say to fix them?"

"Run the hook under the big fin on the back."

"How's that?" queried Owen, holding up the baited hook.

"It looks all right, but I don't know how it will work," said Martin.

"We'll soon find that out," replied Owen, casting his line into the stream. "At least, it hasn't frightened them away," he continued, after a short pause, "for one is biting now, and—and—and here it is."

"Yes, here the line is," said Martin, "but both perch and minnow are gone. I see that you don't understand the new way of fishing."

"It is much better to bait them through the mouth."

"That's to be proved," argued Martin, "look at this."

Both hooks were then baited in the new way. Bite—jerk—minnow lost—perch gone; it was all over in less than a minute.

"What'd I tell you?" cried Owen.

"Give them more than one chance! Remember how you wished to leave this place in the morning because the fish didn't run up and bite immediately."

"There are three minnows left; if you wish to feed the perch with them, do so. I've had enough fishing for one day."

Martin selected the largest of the three minnows in the bucket. It proved to be a chub, fat and slimy; one that would disappear, oyster like, down the throat of a perch. An unfortunate gourmand seized it, and was soon placed with the other finny captives.

"That was an accident! You'll not catch another perch!" exclaimed Owen.

"Fine luck you are having, boys," said a voice

from behind, while at the same time a hand was laid upon Owen's shoulder. It was Walter Stayford who thus disturbed the boys in their sport. For hours he listened to their conversation, but so engrossed were they with the perch that not one word was uttered which gave Stayford the least satisfaction. Seeing that they would soon leave the place, he emerged from behind the bushes with the intention of questioning them and discovering whether or not any one in the neighborhood was suspected of illicit distilling. He congratulated Owen on the manly fight which he had made to save the war message, and then, from flattery, went on to ask if anything of importance had happened since the news from the battle. With all his prying and talking, however, he learned nothing. Certainly the boys had not heard of Simpson's adventure, nor was Owen aware that Tom the Tinker was the man who had sought to gain possession of the message.

While not altogether satisfactory, and of a negative character, the results of the meagre knowledge which Stayford thus obtained, were not without their importance. The fact that Simpson had been detected in delivering the whisky and had been pursued was not generally known, for, if so, the boys would certainly have heard some of the neighbors speak of it. This was good news. Yet it was just possible that those who were in possession of the secret pretended to know nothing of the matter, so as to facilitate the capture of the men who had sold the whisky. Such were the thoughts which Stayford revolved in his mind as he stood talking to the boys on the river bank. Nothing could now be done but return to the cave and wait for the stage. Jerry was right; no doubt, if any effort was being made to capture the illicit distillers, the men thus engaged were in correspondence with Squire Grundy.

CHAPTER XXI.

Mr. Lane has a Difficulty.

"**G**OOD MORNING, Mr. Lane," said Squire Grundy, thrusting his huge, shaggy head through the stage door and grasping the giant's hand.

"Good morning, Squire! Step right in; we have just room for one more."

"That's lucky, Mr. L——beg your pardon, sir; beg your pardon. You see, this is the first time we have met since you were made sheriff of Nelson County. Have you grown any larger since you became sheriff?" asked the Squire, taking a seat by the side of Mr. Lane.

"Not any larger, but a little wiser, I reckon."

"We are never too old to learn, Mr. Lane—beg your pardon again, Sheriff—we are never too old to learn. I've been a justice of the peace for long on eighteen years, and I learn something new every day."

"Did you ever learn that you were not fit for your office?" inquired Mr. Lane.

"I did not come in here to be insulted—I won't take an insult from any man, even if he is the biggest in the State!" said the indignant Squire, rising to his feet, throwing his broad-brimmed hat on the back of his head and resting on his large, home-made cane.

"How have I insulted you?"

"You called in question, sir, my capabilities of administering the responsible and official duties of a Justice of the Peace," continued the Squire, hoping by this display of learning to confound the ignorant sheriff.

In this he succeeded. The half-dozen passengers stared at the Squire in admiration and astonishment, while the discomfited sheriff wondered what he had said to thus enrage old Grundy.

"All aboard!" shouted a voice from without. At the same instant the stage gave a sudden lunge forward. The grave and portly Squire, losing his balance, fell toward Mr. Lane, who reached out his powerful arm and caught him.

"Stop the stage!" cried out the unlucky man, regaining his feet and wiping the perspiration from his forehead. "Stop the stage until I give that driver some advice. Starting at a run before giving his passengers notice!"

Thump! thump! went the wheels against a large stone. The Squire again came down from his tragic position; but he was fortunate enough this time to fall back into the seat from which he had arisen. He continued to talk and thunder against the driver, while the stage continued to roll and thunder over the rough road until Bardstown was far behind.

"Sheriff Lane," said the Squire, recalling the subject of conversation, which he had entirely forgotten in his rage against the driver, "I want it understood that I am profoundly and adequately capable of fulfilling the manifold and important duties of my office."

"And what I want to say is this," replied Mr. Lane, himself becoming irritated, "I am not fit for the office of sheriff of Nelson County."

"And you said, sir, that I was not fit for my office."

"I did not, Squire."

"You did, Sheriff."

"I tell you, I did not."

"I tell you, you did."

"I was going to talk about myself. I was going to say that I was not the man for sheriff. Before I had time to say it you jumped to your feet and stopped me."

"Then it was all a mistake, Sheriff. Let us shake hands and be friends."

"And why do you think that you are not the right man for sheriff?" asked old Grundy after the reconciliation.

"In the first place, I can't read much and can't write."

"Not at all necessary for your work as sheriff. A man in my position as justice of the peace should be profoundly educated. But for your work, Sheriff, what is wanted is a brave man and a sharp man."

"That's just the difficulty; I am not a sharp man—I am not."

"Why do you say that?"

Mr. Lane did not answer. He looked at the other passengers, not one of whom was apparently listening to the conversation. Evidently he had something to communicate to the Squire which he did not want known to his traveling companions, for he whispered to him a few words, after which the two men left their places and took seats on the top of the stage.

"Well, Squire," said Mr. Lane, who was the first to speak, "this is strange work for me. You see, Mr. Pense was sheriff of the county, and Mud was deputy. Mr. Pense died, Mr. Mud became sheriff, and I was made deputy. Then Mr. Mud died and I was made sheriff. It all happened in less than a month. I didn't want the office, but everybody wanted me to take it, and I said yes. The very next day I got some work to do, which has kept me busy for nearly four weeks, and I am just as far off the track to-day as when I started."

Mr. Lane then gave a long account of the work in which he had been engaged. It seems that the men who followed Simpson on the morning after the celebration of the victory of New Orleans saw nothing extraordinary in his actions. Afterwards, however, when talking about the matter, they wondered why he had abandoned his team. Certainly, he thought that he was pursued. He made every effort to escape his pursuers. Finding it impossible, he leaped from his wagon and fled into the woods. What could be the cause of these strange proceedings? After considering the matter for some time, they concluded that there was but one—the man was delivering illicit whisky. He was frightened when he saw the men coming in full gallop after him, and saved himself by flight. This explained everything fully; without it his whole action was a mystery. The sheriff was made aware of the facts by one who hoped to receive a reward in case of an arrest.

To track the man and his accomplices seemed to be an easy task; for, if once the wagon was found, the owner could be identified. A plain case—so plain to Mr. Lane's mind that he started at once for Bardstown without asking any assistance. The wagon and team, however, as has been seen, had been stolen. After a fruitless effort of two days' the inexperienced sheriff called others to his aid; but with all their prying and probing, no clue to the mystery could be found. The case was finally abandoned. Mr. Lane was returning home.

For more than an hour Mr. Grundy listened to the recital of these events, interrupting the speaker at intervals, explaining how he would have acted under the circumstances, suggesting methods which might still prove successful, and giving much wholesome advice which might prove of service to the sheriff in his future official career. While they were still conversing, the stage descended a steep grade into a ravine, over which the massive forest trees interlaced their branches, forming a gloomy and perpetual twilight.

*　　*　　*　　*　　*　　*

There was one apartment in the cave with which the reader has not yet been made familiar. Jerry gave it the name of the "hold out," for here it was that he and Stayford spent most of their time. The "hold out" enjoyed the luxury of a glass window of no mean dimensions, being the only part of the cave which received the light of the sun. The main entrance to the cave, as has already been seen, faced the river toward the south; the ledge of rocks came to an abrupt termination about forty feet farther on toward the west, and it was near this point that the window looked over a wide, deep valley. Jerry accidentally discovered that the rock was very thin at this one place, and by patient care cut through it and admitted the sunlight into the gloomy dwelling. The window was concealed by large grapevines, carefully trained so as to cut off the view from below, without at the same time obstructing the light. This arrangement enabled the two men to spend days and weeks in their natural abode without once leaving it.

Here it is that we find them busily engaged in their preparations for intercepting the mail. Stayford was sitting upon a bed constructed of roughly hewn branches covered with straw, and was carefully loading his two pistols. Jerry occupied a stool in the middle of the "hold out," adjusting a mask made of deer-skin.

"How's that?" he inquired, when the mask had been arranged to his satisfaction.

"Improves your looks very much," replied Stayford; "advise you to wear one all the time."

"And how's that?" again inquired Jerry, turning his coat inside out and pulling his hat down over his eyes.

"Still improved."

"And how's that?" he asked a third time, securing his heavy pistols around his waist and hanging a keen hunting knife at his left side.

"Why, old fellow, it looks as if you were going to fight."

"No; I ain't goin' to fight nobody. I ain't goin' to kill nobody. I won't steal nothin' but mail. We'll just see if thare's a letter for Squire Grundy; and if thare ain't, well, we'll let the mail go, and the stage go."

"You're right, Jerry; we won't take a cent. Robbing and stealing are not in our line. We'll leave that kind of work to such men as Tom the Tinker."

When their preparations were completed the two men left the cave for their hazardous adventure.

CHAPTER XXII.

Mr. Lane Finds a Solution to His Difficulty.

"HERE, BOUNCE! Here Bounce!" called Owen in a loud voice as he rushed from the house, rifle in hand, crossed the barnyard, and ran at full speed toward a strip of woods which joined with the forest. "Here, Bounce!" he continued to call, looking back now and then to see whether the dog was following. But Bounce was in the field with the negro workmen, too far away to hear the voice of his master.

At the edge of the woods Owen found the mangled body of a young lamb. Glancing down a narrow ravine, he saw a wildcat disappear in the thick underbrush not two hundred yards away. This was the marauder for which the boy was looking. It had stolen into the sheep-fold and made off with a lamb in the full light of day.

Owen gave one more anxious look to see whether Bounce was near, then turned and plunged into the woods in pursuit of the bold robber. He shouted as he ran, hoping thereby to frighten the wildcat and force it to climb a tree, when it would be an easy mark for his rifle. But the cat was too experienced a thief to be entrapped so easily. Had Bounce been there he would have driven it into the position Owen wished it. The boy, however, moved too slowly to bring it to bay. For an instant he saw its long, lithe body as the animal leaped upon the trunk of a fallen sycamore, gave a piteous cry and then disappeared again farther down in the ravine.

To run after it or to shout would only terrify it the more. Owen therefore changed his tactics. He left the ravine and walked slowly along the hillside for nearly a mile, pausing every few minutes to examine the tops of the trees, especially those of the tall poplars which seemed to offer a safe hiding place. The pursuit was brought to an abrupt termination by a steep cliff which overlooked the old stage road. A dark object was seen moving among the brush just below him. The boy raised his rifle in readiness to fire, but the undergrowth was so thick that he could not see distinctly. He changed his position and looked again; it was not a wildcat. But what could the object be? A goat? No; there was not one in the neighborhood; besides, the head was more than five feet from the ground. Further inspection showed that the object was a man. Two were there, partly concealed by the bushes. They had masks of rough deer-skin pulled over their faces. This it was that gave the first one the appearance of a goat.

But what were these two men waiting for? Why had they concealed themselves here so close to the road? After a moment's reflection Owen concluded that they intended to rob the stage. They could certainly have chosen no better spot, as it was fully a mile away from the nearest farmhouse and in a place where the stage would necessarily move slowly. The men were well armed; they had posted themselves, too, within ten feet of the road, where they could both spring forward in front of the stage.

Something must be done to give the travelers warning! So thought Owen as he crept away from the cliff. Perhaps the best plan would be to run some distance up the road, wait for the stage, and tell the driver what he had seen. As he paused for a few seconds to deliberate he heard the old stage rumbling down the hillside not a quarter of a mile away. To reach it now and give warning of the danger was impossible, for it was on the opposite side of the ravine. All that he could do was to wait until the stage hove in sight, then yell and fire his rifle to frighten the robbers and let them know that their movements had been watched. On the other hand, he would be perfectly safe; for he could make his escape before the two men had time to climb the steep cliff and pursue him. Owen crawled back to a position where he could watch the bandits without being seen by them.

In the meantime, lumbering slowly along the rough road into the deep ravine, came the old stage, on whose top were two travelers whom Owen recognized as his old friend Coon-Hollow Jim and Squire Grundy. The Squire was gesticulating and talking vociferously in vain endeavors to be heard above the noise of the grinding wheels. Ostensibly he was entertaining the new sheriff; but he was aware of the fact that two lady passengers below were listening to him as he recounted his many deeds of valor in the Indian wars.

He was suddenly interrupted by a scream from one of the ladies as the two robbers stepped forward and ordered the driver to dismount and unhitch his horses. It was no small humiliation for the new sheriff and the boastful Squire when told to take their places near the stage driver and hold their hands above their heads. With them were two other men, the women and three children being left undisturbed. One of the bandits placed himself before the five men, and, pistol in hand, threatened to blow out the brains of the first that attempted to escape, while the other forced the mail-bag open and began to examine its contents.

Squire Grundy trembled from head to foot, for he feared that his guard's pistol, which was pointed at his head, might go off at any minute. Coon-Hollow Jim stood sullen and stolid; he felt that he was more than a match for the two robbers, yet in his present position he was powerless.

But where was Owen? Why did he not give the alarm as he had resolved to do? So frightened and bewildered was he that he remained for some time a passive spectator of the scene. Finally he regained his courage and resolved to assist his old friend Coon-Hollow Jim. Yet which should he do? To kill or wound the robber—his mind revolted from such a plan. To shoot the pistol from his hand—this was an easy task, though to hit it in such a way as to make the ball glance off without the least danger to the passengers—this required the perfection of his skill, but this he resolved to do.

Never did Owen's rifle-craft prove more useful to him than at that moment. Conscious of his power, he raised his rifle. His aim was long and true and steady. Then a sharp, clear ring, followed by the deep, loud report of the highwayman's pistol, discharged by the shock of his bullet. For a moment both robbers and passengers were dazed. No one seemed to know what had happened or to have noticed that a rifle had been fired. But the bewilderment was only for a moment.

Mr. Lane, seeing his guard unarmed and helpless, sprang toward him and seized him in his iron grasp. The other bandit, too, was soon overpowered and made a prisoner.

"Hold them tight! Hold them tight! Ropes to bind them! Ropes to bind them!" exclaimed the excited

Squire, keeping at a safe distance from the two robbers.

The driver bound the hands of the two prisoners behind them with strong hemp rope.

"The rogues and thieves!" continued the Squire with much indignation. "The country is full of them! It's as dangerous to travel now as when we had the Indians around, forty years ago!"

As soon as the prisoners were secured all fell to praising Mr. Lane for his bravery. For, in their opinion, he had suddenly sprung upon the highwayman, knocked the pistol from his hands and made him a prisoner.

"That's the boldest, bravest deed that I've witnessed in all my wide experience," said the Squire. "To attack an armed robber who holds a pistol at your breast, to overpower him and take him prisoner unaided—that, sir, is something that has never been done before in this State or country. Then to dodge the bullet! Sheriff, how you dodged the bullet when he fired at you is more than I can understand. I predict a unanimous vote for you in the next election—a unanimous vote, sir. For when the people hear of this day's work they'll have no one else for sheriff of Nelson County." The Squire would have talked for half an hour, but the driver interrupted him, and insisted on starting at once.

The two prisoners were made to take seats on the top of the stage, where Mr. Lane, pistol in hand, sat to guard them; and in a few moments the coach and four disappeared over the hill beyond the ravine. The passengers congratulated themselves on their fortunate escape, little dreaming of the part which Owen had played in the capture of the robbers.

Owen, too, was pleased with the turn which events had taken. His first impulse was to call out to the travelers and explain why the pistol had dropped from the bandit's hand; but when he noted their praise for Mr. Lane, and heard Squire Grundy say that his bravery would win for him the vote of every man in the county, Owen determined then and there to let no one know that a shot from his rifle had brought so much honor on his friend.

For an hour or more neither of the prisoners spoke a word. They wore their masks, too, so that Mr. Lane was ignorant of the fact that the fleshy man before him was the jolly fiddler and marksman whom he had met at the famous shooting-match on Grundy's farm.

Within the stage, the Squire was entertaining the passengers with stories of Indian wars. He had often seen Indians dodge bullets, but Mr. Lane, he thought, was the first white man to perform such a feat. The sheriff was elated as he listened to these words of praise from so great and influential a man as Squire Grundy. In the meantime, he carelessly examined the pistol which he held in his hand. Something had struck the upper part of the rusty barrel; the mark looked like one made by a bullet. Was not this the pistol, too, that had fallen from the robber's hand? While the sheriff was thinking over the matter and trying to find some connection between the mark and the surprise of the prisoners, one of the bandits spoke to him.

"I don't wish," said he, "to ask for anything either for myself or my partner. We've been caught robbing a stage, and must serve our term in the penitentiary; but there is another man in this work, and he must come with us."

"That's right," chimed in his companion, from beneath his mask. "Catch that devil of a Tinker, and you can have all three of us. Me and this hare feller was nothin' but rabbits for goin' into this hare work, and we desarve to be caught in our own traps."

"We didn't intend to rob the stage," continued the first speaker.

"That there may be true," interrupted the sheriff, "but I reckon the law won't look at it in that there way."

"I know it won't! I know it won't!" said the prisoner. "Remember, I'm not asking for mercy; only listen to what I have to say, and when you've heard all you'll believe me."

Here the stage drew up in front of the Grundy homestead, an old manor, approached by an avenue of silver poplars, and surrounded by a wide veranda. The Squire bade the passengers good-bye, assuring them at the same time that they were perfectly safe in the company of so brave a man as Sheriff Lane.

"What I have to say is this," resumed the prisoner, when the stage was under way again. "We are not highway robbers. For years we've lived in this part of the country, worked and trapped, and injured no one. But a scoundrel and thief, whom we call Tom the Tinker, persuaded us to go into the whisky business. For three years we made whisky in a cave on the bank of the Beech Fork, about six miles from here. Then we were caught; at least, we thought so. Our object in stopping the stage to-day was to see whether any notice had been sent to Squire Grundy or the sheriff about the matter. You notice that we did not attempt to rob the passengers. Instead of finding the letters, we met the Squire and yourself. I didn't know at the time that you were sheriff, but, sheriff or not, we had you just where we wanted you until my pistol went off and fell from my hand. How it happened, I don't know. We're your prisoners, and'll be sent up for five years. But we must have Tom the Tinker with us."

"What made you suspect that your plans were discovered?" asked the sheriff.

"We sent six barrels to Bardstown."

"When?"

"The day after the news from New Orleans."

"And the driver was foller'd?"

"Yes."

"And left that there team on the road?"

"Yes; he jumped from the wagon when the men came near him, and made his way back to the cave on foot."

"Where's the wagon?"

"Don't know, sir."

"I've been lookin' for that there wagon for two weeks."

"The wagon belonged to the Tinker," said the prisoner. "He's the cause of our ruin, and he must come to the penitentiary with us."

He then proceeded to give the sheriff an accurate description of the cave, with minute details in regard to the path which led to it. The Tinker must be arrested while actually engaged in making whisky; this would ensure him a sentence of ten years in the penitentiary.

All that day Mr. Lane talked with the prisoner about the capture of Tom the Tinker and the destruction of the illicit distillery. The second prisoner spoke but little. Only after it was quite dark, and the stage approached Louisville, did he remove his mask and make known to his captor who he was. It was a painful task for the good-natured sheriff to hand over the jolly fiddler and marksman to the jail authorities; yet this was his duty, and he did not shrink from it.

"I'll expect to see the Tinker with us before two weeks have passed," said Stayford, as the sheriff turned to leave the jail.

"Yes! bring him on," said Jerry, "and then you can hang all three of us. We is darned fools for bein' caught in our own traps, and desarve to be hanged."

CHAPTER XXIII.

The Mark on Stayford's Pistol.

THE STAGE was on its return trip from Louisville. It had but a single passenger, and that passenger was Sheriff Lane, who sat with the driver on top of the coach. The conversation naturally drifted to the capture of the two robbers the previous week. The driver said that he had thought the matter over for hours at a time, and had but one solution to the strange conduct of Stayford. The man, he thought, was not accustomed to such work; he grew nervous under the strain, and accidentally fired the revolver, on which he had but a slight hold. In consequence of this, it rebounded from his hand.

"I've been thinking that there matter over," said Mr. Lane, at the same time drawing from his pocket the identical pistol which Stayford had dropped. "Do you see that there mark on the upper part of the rusty barrel?" he asked, as he held up the weapon in front of the driver.

"Plainly," was the answer.

"What do you think done it?"

"It seems to be the mark of a bullet."

"When do you think that there mark was made?"

"Certainly within the past few days."

"So far we agree exactly," said the sheriff. "I noticed that there mark about an hour after I arrested the robbers. It was somewhat brighter then than it is now. I reckon that a rifle shot from the top of the hill knocked that there pistol from Stayford's hand. What's your opinion?"

"In the first place, Sheriff, we should have heard the report of the rifle."

"That's my only difficulty," put in Mr. Lane. "But we'll settle that there thing later on. What else have you to say?"

"Well, I reckon any sensible fellow would shoot at the robber, and not at the robber's pistol."

"Most fellers would! Most fellers would!" repeated the sheriff. "But I know one feller that wouldn't— young Howard, who won the prize at Grundy's farm last fall. You see, he's only a boy, and he would not care about shootin' nobody. But he knew that he could hit that pistol clean and sharp; and he's the only feller in this here part of the country who could do it. Did you ever hear of young Howard?"

"I reckon I didn't," remarked the driver.

"Then half of your life is lost, my friend."

"Does he shoot well?"

"Shoot! Great pos-sim-mons! Shoot!" exclaimed Mr. Lane. "Every time that there boy raises his rifle somethin' drops; I never seen the like of it in my born days!"

"So you think that young Howard happened to be on the bluff overlooking the road."

"He was up there, sure as a gun. He's the only one who could have done the work so clean and sharp. Just look at this," continued the sheriff, as he held the pistol in front of the driver. "Just look at this mark! The ball struck the barrel in exactly the right spot. Had the boy missed his aim the width of a straw he would either have failed to knock the pistol from Stayford's hand or would have run the risk of killing one of us."

"But why didn't the little fellow show himself?" asked the driver.

"I reckon he's kind of scared, and made off for home. He ain't one of them here fellers that puts on much. Down at Grundy's, when he had won in the wing shot, I had hard work getting him to try at the target. You see, he missed the target first, because his powder was wet. But when he did begin shooting—great pos-sim-mons! he just done the best I ever seen! He drove the ball home to the bull's eye every crack!"

"But again I ask, Sheriff, why did we not hear the rifle?"

"I reckon that's hard to explain. But I'll ask the boy what happened when he fired. I'm going to get off at Howard's and stay around that part of the country for a week or so. I have important business there."

"Something connected with the elections, I reckon," said the driver.

"Them elections is a long ways off. Still, I reckon I'll run when the time comes. With Squire Grundy on my side, I ought to make a tol'able good fight."

The men continued to talk about the robbers and the elections until they came to a station, where the horses were exchanged and several passengers taken in.

It was a little before sunset when the stage drew up in front of the Howard homestead. What was Owen's surprise, when, looking through the window of the dining-room, he saw his giant friend entering the yard gate, while the stage continued on its way. This meant that Mr. Lane was to remain at his father's house at least for one night. But what could be the object of his visit? Was he coming to thank Owen for assisting him in capturing the robbers? No! this could not be; for the boy was convinced that no one had seen him or was aware of his presence on that eventful day.

Mr. Howard stepped out on the porch to welcome the stranger.

"Good evening, sir," he said to Mr. Lane, as the latter walked up the narrow foot path toward the house.

"Good even, sir. My name's Dick Lane—Coon-Hollow Jim, the folks often call me. I've got business in this here part of the country, and want to ask if I'll be welcome under your roof for one night."

"For a dozen nights, Mr. Lane—just as long as you wish to stay with us," said the farmer, grasping the visitor's hand. "We've heard of you before, sir," he continued. "Owen often speaks of your kindness to him at the shooting-match."

"He desarved it all, Mr. Howard. A fine lad he is; and the best marksman in the State."

"He does handle a rifle fairly well; but I've had him at the axe and plow for some months past," observed the farmer with a laugh.

"Here's my young friend!" exclaimed the giant, as Owen stepped out on the porch and the two shook hands. "See here, youngster," he continued, "I'm sheriff of the county now, and I think I'll arrest you for beating me at the shooting-match."

"And how do you like your new office?" asked Mr. Howard.

"Only tol'ably well, sir. But I reckon I'll get into it later on."

Bertha appeared at the door and with a courtesy invited the gentlemen in to supper. When the meal was over the two men lighted their cob pipes, and, at Mr. Lane's suggestion, strolled out into the woodyard for a private talk. Here they sat for an hour while Mr. Lane explained the object of his visit. He gave the whole history of the whisky cave, told of the arrest of Jerry and Stayford, and finally declared his intention of proceeding to the cave on the following morning, in the hope of arresting Tom the Tinker while the latter was actually engaged in making whisky.

"Now I understand all," said Mr. Howard, when he had listened to the visitor's story; "I knew there was a thief in this part of the country; I suspected the man, but I could never put my finger on any one. Tom the Tinker was certainly a clever man; but all thieves and robbers are caught in the end. His time has now come."

The two men sat in silence for some time, watching the smoke as it curled up from their glowing pipes.

"But Jerry," resumed the farmer in a low, sad voice; "I'm sorry for Jerry. He's been a dear, good friend of us all for these many years. How the young folks will miss him—will miss his fiddle—his jolly call at the dance; still, I see no way to help him now; he's been caught, and must abide by his sentence."

"I found it hard to give him over to the jailer," added Mr. Lane, "but my duty called for it."

"That it did, Sheriff; you would not have been the man for your office if you had let him escape. We must often do things that are not pleasant."

The two men arose and walked slowly toward the house. Mr. Howard volunteered to assist the Sheriff, but the latter preferred to make the arrest alone. It was his intention to start for the cave early on the following morning, so as to examine the entrance during the day and be ready to capture the Tinker at night.

Mr. Howard brought the visitor to Owen's room, where a bed had been prepared for him. As soon as the farmer retired, the sheriff drew Stayford's pistol from his pocket, and, handing it to Owen, asked whether he had ever seen it before.

The boy examined the rusty weapon, then gave it back with the assurance that this was the first time he had seen it.

"Take it again, and look at the barrel," said Mr. Lane.

Owen was still ignorant of the fact that this was the pistol which he had knocked from Stayford's hand; but as he inspected it closely the truth forced itself upon him—that indentation in the middle of the barrel had been made by his rifle. He was not surprised that the sheriff should have kept the robber's revolver, but why did he insist on Owen's examining it?

"Come, my boy," said the sheriff, "is there no strange mark on that there barrel?"

"A small one, just in the center."

"Something like a bullet mark, I reckon."

"Yes, sir," said Owen, with a laugh, for he now began to suspect that either Mr. Lane or some of the other travelers had seen him when he stepped from behind the tree to fire at Stayford's pistol.

"Oh, you little rascal! You beat me at the shooting-match last fall, but I reckon I've got you now. A bullet from your rifle made that there mark." The sheriff laughed, and so did Owen.

The latter then explained how he chanced to be in the woods that day, and how, by accident, he had observed the two robbers. He acknowledged, too, that a shot from his rifle had rescued Mr. Lane and the other travelers from the hands of the robbers.

"Why did you not let us know that you were up on that hill?" asked the sheriff.

"One good turn deserves another," said Owen, hesitatingly. "You helped me at the shooting-match; I helped you to capture the robbers. That made us even; So I thought that I'd say nothing about it."

"But it's strange that none of us heard the crack of your rifle."

"I scarcely heard it myself," was the boy's reply. "It seemed to me that my rifle and the robber's pistol went off at the same time."

"Won't Squire Grundy be surprised when he hears how it all happened?" said Mr. Lane.

He was certainly a happy man that night. He had not only proved that he was brave, but, by discovering the part which Owen had taken in the capture of the robbers he showed beyond a doubt that he could knit facts together in such a way as to trace out accomplices, even where the shrewd Squire failed to do so.

Owen soon found himself talking with the visitor as familiarly as if the two were on terms of equality, and had been friends for years.

"Do you know what Father Byrne called you and

me when he heard that I was going to the shooting-match?" he asked.

"You mean that sort of a preacher what comes 'round here?" said the sheriff.

"Yes, sir; the priest. We call him Father to show our respect for him."

"I seen him down on the Green river, long on five years ago. He come into Medley's store tol'ably late one night, and was half froze—had been out some forty miles or so to see a sick person. Medley, he's a Catholic, and kept the preacher over all night. He set down at the stove and began to tell us stories. He beats all I've seen for that kind of work, even Squire Grundy, 'cept he didn't lie like the squire. Well, what did the preacher say about you and me and the shootin'-match?"

"He called me David, and you Goliath."

"Go-go-who?"

"Goliath—the big man—the giant."

"Live 'round this here part of the country?" inquired Mr. Lane.

"No-o-o-o!" exclaimed Owen, with a prolonged and evident surprise.

"Never heard of him before," said the visitor.

"Father Byrne brought me a book which tells all about David and Goliath. Here it is," he continued, as he took a small illustrated Bible history from a table and held it in the dim light of a tallow candle.

"Go-go-what's his name?"

"Goliath."

"Go-go-li-yah is one of them there fellers you read about in books. That's the reason I didn't know nothin' about him. You see, I can't read much, my lad. Squire Grundy says I'm got to larn better, and how to write, too, before the next election. But now, just tell me about the Go-go-li-yah."

"He was a very big man—a giant," began Owen. "David was a small boy. The two had a fight, and the little boy killed the big giant."

"And that's the reason the preacher called me Go-go-li-yah," said Mr. Lane; "because I was a big man, and was whipped by you. But what did old Go-li-yah fight with—a horse-pistol, I reckon?"

"N-o-o-o," replied Owen, with another prolonged surprise. "Goliath used a sword, and David a sling."

"One of them things that boys use for throwing rocks?" inquired Mr. Lane.

"Yes, sir. But here's a picture of the fight. You see, here's the giant lying on his back. David has taken Goliath's sword and has raised it to cut off his head."

"Served him right," answered the visitor, calmly. "If he'd only had sense enough to use a rifle or a ho'se-pistol he wouldn't have had his darn noggle chopped off."

Owen continued to turn the pages of the history slowly, while he narrated some of the striking events of the Old and New Testament. Mr. Lane listened with the simplicity of a child. How he marveled at the passage of the Red Sea—the pillar of fire and luminous cloud in the desert—the fall of the walls of Jericho.

Before retiring that night Owen knelt by his bed and prayed fervently for Mr. Lane; prayed that He who had opened a way through the waters and had lit up the path in the desert would also give to his friend the gift and light of faith.

CHAPTER XXIV.

Tom the Tinker.

"GOOD LUCK to you, my friend!" said Mr. Howard, as he accompanied Mr. Lane to the yard gate and pointed out the path which led down to the river. "But be careful, sir; be careful. Remember that you are dealing with a villain—he is not a murderer; at least, I never heard of his killing any one—but he is cruel—as cruel a man as ever came to this State. I do believe that he would shoot down anyone who dared come between him and his money. But remember, too, that he is a coward. He'll not meet you face to face. Once you've captured him, watch him closely, for I fear that he'll attempt to take his own life when he sees that he has fallen into the hands of the law."

"I'm new at this business, as you know, Mr. Howard. Luck has been with me so far, and I hope it will stay. This here is sartin; if I don't capture Tom the Tinker it won't be because I didn't do my part. Good morning, sir!"

"Good morning!"

"If I get the Tinker it will be a good shot for me in the next election for sheriff." With these words Mr. Lane started off on his perilous mission.

The farmer stood and watched him until he disappeared, and then turned and walked slowly toward the house, muttering as he went: "The villain! the villain! If he is not captured this time, then I'll take a hand in the fight!"

Mr. Lane strode along the river bank, pushing his way through the patches of horse-weed which grew quite close to the water's edge. He did not follow the path farther up on the hill, as he did not wish to be observed. He often paused to mark his way, for he thought that it would be necessary for him to retrace his steps at night.

High above his head, on the bare limbs of a sycamore, a restive rain-crow croaked—its call predicting heavy rains and bad luck. The old marksman raised his rifle with deadly aim toward the rufous-winged prophet, held it there for a single second, then, lowering it again, said, "If I'd only pulled the trigger, my little friend, you'd never bring bad luck to nobody again."

A strange feeling came over him as he drew near the cave, so that he used every means to divert his mind. He spoke to the clattering kingfishers, even though they had no inclination to tarry with him; he gazed at the stupid frogs along the river bank; he watched the tanagers which seemed like balls of fire among the green foliage of the trees. The closer he came to his destination the slower he walked; as a consequence, it was almost mid-day when he stood before the two giant rocks, the guardian genii of that mysterious place.

With his right hand grasping his revolver, he passed cautiously through the narrow entrance. Here he paused and listened, but heard nothing. With difficulty he found the rock door. It seemed but a part of the solid stone wall, with a slight, irregular fracture along the side. It was in a dark corner, too, where the light from without did not penetrate. The sheriff drew from his pocket two keys, if keys they could be called, for they were simply pieces of seasoned hickory about ten inches in length, so shaped as to lift a latch. With the largest of these the door was opened. Through it he went into the chamber where Martin and Owen had been held as prisoners on that eventful October night, and again he paused and listened, but still heard nothing. Only the faintest light from without was admitted here, but enough for Mr. Lane to see that he had not reached the place where whisky was made. The walls were no longer decorated with the skins of wild animals. As no fire had been lighted there for weeks, the air was damp and chilly.

The sheriff suddenly recollected that Stayford had spoken to him of two passages leading from this second room, and had directed him to take the one opposite the rock door. He lit a firebrand which he had brought and walked toward this second entrance. He was convinced by this time that no one was in the cave; besides, Jerry had assured him that neither the Tinker nor Simpson ever remained there during the day.

The whisky still was found, and near it several barrels full of mash. The furnace was warm, and, although the fire beneath it had been extinguished, it was evident that someone had been working there during the previous night. It was equally evident that they would return to complete their labor.

Mr. Lane had intended to examine the cave closely, but not to stay there until dark. His plan was to conceal himself in the woods, watch the men when they entered and then follow them. Now, however, he concluded that it was better to remain in the cave, as he could easily find a hiding place.

At one end of the room in which the whisky was made was a passage leading into the "hold out." The sheriff took from his pocket a second key, unlocked the door, and went into the former dwelling place of Jerry the Trapper. This door could be bolted from within, and so firmly that it was impossible to force an entrance without breaking the solid rock slab of which it was made. Mr. Lane decided to wait here until Simpson and the Tinker returned to the cave, and turned the heavy bolt.

The new occupant then began to examine the contents of his strange abode. At one side hung an iron lamp, with just a little tallow in it. Scattered on the floor were deer-skin leggings and moccasins, caps, and jackets of home-spun, just as Jerry had left them a few days before, when he was preparing for the stage robbery. There were various devices used for cooking utensils. But what interested the sheriff most were the instruments for cutting stone. They were of the very finest material, and had evidently been brought from England. With them the old trapper had cut the two massive doors, and had also opened a way from the side of the cave through which to introduce corn and wood and to roll out the barrels of whisky. Then there was the small window with a single pane of glass; the whole being ingeniously covered by wild grapevines which Jerry had trained along the ledge without.

After Mr. Lane had examined everything in the little room the passing hours became long and tiresome. The little window gradually lost its light, until finally all around was shrouded in darkness. With the night came a protracted vigilance on the part of the sheriff. Mr. Lane sat close to the rock door which he had opened and kept a few inches ajar. At length he heard footsteps at the entrance of the cave. He closed the door, and waited, for he wished to give the Tinker time to begin his work.

When ten minutes had passed he cocked his revolver, threw open the door, and rushed from the "hold out."

All was darkness, everywhere perfect quiet. Not a person! not a sound! For a moment the sheriff stood as if petrified, then turned and groped his way back into the "hold out."

With his flint he lighted a firebrand, then returned to examine the cave. In one of the narrow passages he found a place which seemed to have been recently disturbed; this he examined closely. A large fragment of a stone had fallen away from the mother rock and had crushed down the rough sides. It was this noise, no doubt, which he had heard, and had mistaken for footsteps. Back to the "hold out" he went again. The rest of that night and the following day dragged on slowly, Mr. Lane sleeping but little.

Just as it was growing dusk on the second day, he determined to take a short rest. When he awoke it was quite bright. He sat up, and rubbed his eyes, and wondered what had happened. Could it be possible that he had slept during the entire night? He unbolted the door and went out into the cave. Things had been changed there. Some barrels had been filled and others emptied, and there was a smouldering fire under the simmering still.

The sheriff was not discouraged. As several barrels of mash remained, one or two nights would be required to boil them down. From the amount of work done during the preceding night, he judged that two men at most had been there, and these two would, no doubt, return to finish the work. True, he would have to wait another day, but this seemed little to him now that he felt so sure of capturing the Tinker and his companion. Before the day had passed he ate the last of his provisions, smoked his last pipeful of tobacco; then sought to take another rest, as he felt confident that he would have to stand guard over his prisoners during the greater part of the night.

At one end of the "hold out" there was a ledge of rock protruding so far that it formed a natural bed, where he could rest without being seen, even if any one entered the room. With difficulty the sheriff mounted up into this hard bed, and soon was fast asleep.

He was awakened by an explosion like the crash of an earthquake. He sprang up suddenly, hitting the top of the cave with such force that he fell back half unconscious. As he gradually recovered he heard the sound of voices below.

"What would Jerry say," asked one, "if he knew that we had blasted the rock door into fragments?"

"Jerry is in jail," said the other, with a growl. "Jerry is in jail; I hope he will stay there. All that I want is his money. He never spent any. I wonder where he hid it?"

"What part am I to get?" asked the first speaker, as the two began to search among the old clothes and in crevices in the rocks.

"We'll settle that when we find the money."

"We'll settle it now. How much am I to get?"

"You'll be satisfied with—"

"One-half."

"What, Simpson! You want one-half—a half!"

"Yes, a half."

"But you didn't work for it; it came from my corn and my whisky."

"It belongs to Jerry now. If we find it, we take one-half each."

"Wants one-half of it, my! my!"

"Yes, one-half."

"Won't a fourth do?"

"No!"

"Nor a third?"

"No! no!"

"My! my! my!"

"See, here! Tom! I'm the only man left to help you to do your work. Before I begin I must have the promise of half of Jerry's money. One-half, or you'll not make another drop of whisky in this cave!"

"My! my! my! my!" whined the old miser.

Simpson made no reply. He sat down on one of the benches and looked straight into the Tinker's face.

Tom continued to whimper, but he saw that Simpson was firm, so he assented to his terms.

"Can't help it."

"Now that we have begun to make terms," continued Simpson, "let me tell you what I must have of all the whisky we sell. One-fifth of the profits must be mine."

"One-fifth!" stammered the Tinker.

"Yes, one-fifth."

"One barrel in five!"

"Yes."

"That's more than Jerry got."

"But it is what I must get."

"It's more than Jerry and Stayford got."

"Can't help it."

"It's twice as much as they got."

"But you robbed them; they often told you so, and you know it."

"My! my! my!"

"I'll take one-fifth, and not a cent less!"

"My! my! And now you *are* robbing me!"

"Remember, Tom, the work is more dangerous than it was when Jerry worked with you. You don't know what moment Sheriff Lane might come in here and put his hand on your shoulder."

The old coward was startled, and glanced anxiously from one side to the other.

Mr. Lane the while was anything but comfortable. They were to examine the "hold out" to find Jerry's money; evidently they would climb up to the place where he was lying. Luckily he had carried his two revolvers with him; these he held in his hands ready for action.

The Tinker continued to groan, and curse, and argue with Simpson; but in the end he was forced to yield.

"Now that we have reached a conclusion, let us wait until morning before we search for the money," suggested Simpson.

"I want to see how much there is. I always thought that Jerry was rich," said Tom.

"I hope he was. But the money can keep until

morning; whereas the mash may sour if we don't run it through."

"Just as you say," assented the Tinker. "You're robbing me of half of it anyway, so there won't be much when the sum's divided."

"*Robbing* you!"

"Yes, *robbing* me!"

"You're a liar, Tom. I'm only insisting on my rights."

"You accused *me* of robbing Jerry and Stayford, and now *you* are robbing me."

"The money we are looking for belongs to no one since Jerry is in jail. If we find it I am entitled to one-half."

"Besides, you force me to give you one-fifth of the profits of the whisky—of the whisky I've spent my days and nights in making, into which I have put hundreds of bushels of corn. That's robbing me! That's robbing me!"

"I simply gave you my terms and you agreed to them!"

"I am *forced* to agree."

"You are not!"

"What can I do?"

"Get some one else."

"And have him betray me?"

"I thought that we had already come to an agreement," said Simpson, with some warmth. "Let me repeat here what I said before. I don't intend to risk my life in selling your whisky without being well paid for it."

"Yes, and you want a price that is little less than robbery."

"Then call it robbery; call it what you will. But remember the price remains."

"One-fifth, my! my! It comes high. But I'll stick to my word, Simpson. You are to get your one-fifth. Come," continued he, "let's get to work at the still; for, as you said, the mash may sour, but Jerry's money will keep."

"What is that?" asked Simpson, as he stumbled over something leaning against the side of the "hold out." "Well! well! If it isn't Jerry's old rifle. Leaning there just as natural as if the old trapper was at home."

"Strange he didn't take it with him," replied the Tinker, as he held up his firebrand to examine the old flint lock.

The sheriff was startled, for it was Mr. Howard's rifle, and his name was engraved in large letters on the muzzle. But the Tinker did not examine it carefully, and the two men soon left the "hold out" to begin work at the still.

When the cave began to brighten in the ruddy light from the fire which our two worthies had set vigorously going, Mr. Lane climbed down from his rocky bed and crept carefully toward the door. There he stood for some time where he could observe the men without running any risk of being seen. What a strange, weird sight! They looked like ghosts as they passed to and from the glowing furnace, and their shadows leaped and danced along the walls. Simpson fed the fire and brought the mash, while the Tinker looked after the still and watched the pipes which conducted off the whisky. The sheriff grew so interested in the work that he almost forgot the object of his coming. Were he to seize the men now he could certainly swear that he had captured Tom the Tinker while the latter was making whisky; yet everything seemed so quiet and peaceable that he could with difficulty force himself to begin his disagreeable task. Still now was the time for action. He drew his revolvers and stepped quickly toward the two men.

Imagine the surprise of Simpson and the Tinker when they beheld the giant sheriff stalking forth from the room which they had examined but a few minutes before, his long arms turned menacingly toward them, and his stentorian voice calling on them to surrender. He seemed to them a huge spectre, not a living man. On he came with giant strides, until his revolvers were pointed into their very faces.

"Who are you?" demanded Tom the Tinker, with a show of courage.

"I reckon it don't matter much who I am," replied the sheriff, "but I know who you are. Louis Bowen, you are my prisoner."

CHAPTER XXV.

Off to the Cave.

ON THE EVENING of the third day after the departure of Mr. Lane from the Howard's, Owen was busy at the hand-mill cutting oats for the stock, when Uncle Pius came hobbling into the barn shaking his head in a most mysterious way.

"I know'd it, I know'd it," he muttered, in a low tone, while with solemn steps he paced up and down the barn floor.

"What did you know?" asked Owen, as he made the mill-wheel twirl and buzz, pretending not to be in the least interested in what the old negro had said.

"Can't tell you. Massar said I musn't tell." And Uncle Pius continued his measured steps to and fro, with his head resting upon his breast and his hands clutching his heavy cane behind his back. Owen continued his work. He knew that the best way to get a secret from Uncle Pius was to appear entirely indifferent in regard to it. The old negro walked from one end of the barn to the other several times, then he came to a halt directly in front of Owen.

"I know'd it," he repeated. "I know'd it all 'long. I know'd dar wasn't no corn in dat crib."

The buzz of the mill-wheel was the only answer he received. Uncle Pius turned and started off; but he had not gone ten feet before he retraced his steps.

"I know'd dar wasn't no corn in dat crib. I know'd dar wasn't. I know'd dar wasn't. I'se said so all 'long!" And Uncle Pius brought his massive cane down upon the barn floor.

Still the wheel twirled on; and still Owen was silent.

"Den dat ole Bowen! I know'd he's a rascal. I know'd it all 'long," continued the old negro, becoming more and more excited at every word he uttered.

It was with difficulty that Owen remained silent now. From a few words that his father had dropped at table, he had concluded that Mr. Lane's visit was in some way connected with Louis Bowen. Mr. Lane was sheriff now—had he come to arrest the old villain? But the corn-crib; why did Uncle Pius mention it? The boy's curiosity was soon satisfied; for Uncle Pius had come to tell his story.

The old negro went back to the night of the previous autumn when Bowen's corn-crib had burned. He reminded Owen of the fact that he, Uncle Pius, had stated, and rightly so, that there was no corn in the crib; for old Bowen had hauled it all away to a cave near the river, where, together with two robbers whom Mr. Lane had arrested, he had been making whisky for three years. The two robbers were now in jail, and the sheriff had gone down the river to find the cave and arrest Louis Bowen. But worst of all, as Mr. Lane had promised to return on the second day to get help if he had not succeeded by that time in making the arrest, and had not yet appeared, Mr. Howard was afraid that the sheriff had been killed by the villain.

Owen's heart beat faster and faster as he listened to Uncle Pius; faster and faster, too, in his excitement he made the wheel spin around. Thought after thought rushed through his mind. Mr. Lane was now in Louis Bowen's power—perhaps wounded—perhaps dead. Was there no way to bring him help? Couldn't Owen tell his father that he knew of the cave and persuade him to start at once to rescue Mr. Lane?

But why not go alone? Better still, get Martin Cooper to accompany him. They could reach the cave early in the night and bring assistance to a friend who needed their help. They could frustrate the design of a villain who had sought their lives.

Uncle Pius continued to rehearse his story, changing and distorting facts at each successive repetition. Owen scarcely hearing what the old man said; his mind was too busily engaged in working out a plan of action. As soon as he had made his decision he released his grasp upon the handle of the mill, seized a large willow basket, quickly distributed the oats in the troughs for the horses, leaped from the barn door and ran toward the house. It was lucky for him that he met no one, for his face was flushed with excitement. He took his coat and the pistol which he had won at the shooting-match; passing through the kitchen he thrust a few crusts of bread into his pocket, then dashed off again toward the barn. On his way he met Uncle Pius, who made an ineffectual effort to stop Owen and give him a more detailed account of old Bowen and the cave.

Five minutes later when the old negro saw the boy riding at a breakneck speed across the field toward Martin Cooper's, he shook his head ominously and muttered, "Dat chile am goin' to do somethin' awful. I jes' knows he is!" He had enkindled a fire, but could not quench the flame.

Martin was at supper, but on hearing Owen's familiar call, he went out to the stile-block in front of the yard-gate. The two boys exchanged a few words, and Martin caught his friend's enthusiasm at once. They were not boys who acted without the knowledge and consent of their parents; but on this occasion they were borne away by a sudden impulse and excitement. They consulted no one; they asked no one's permission. In less time than it takes to describe their movements, they had galloped off and disappeared in the gloom of the forest.

The cave! how often had the boys spoken of it, and thought of it, and dreamed of it during the past months! How the secret to which they had pledged themselves burned within their breasts! How they had longed to wander once more through its weird and mazy passages, its dim-lit vaults!

The cave! To enter it in the full light of day, and with the assurance that all was safe within—even this would have been an adventure for the boys—one that past recollections would have clothed with romance. But to penetrate it at night, to stand face to face before a villain whom ill-fortune had made desperate, to rescue Mr. Lane and make old Bowen a prisoner—all this caused the boys' blood to tingle in their veins. Yet it was not the excitement that comes of fear! True, they had quailed before the danger on that October night when Stayford had threatened them with death; but now that friendship called them, with beating hearts and firm resolve they pressed on without a falter.

The cave! Nearer and nearer the boys came to it. At first they spurred their horses and raced along the narrow path by the river bank, but when darkness had enveloped the forest their progress was slow. With difficulty the horses kept the winding road. Dark it was; yet light enough to see the dog-wood, as its long, white branches swayed to and fro in the evening breeze, and appeared like ghosts moving among the shadows of the thick Spring foliage. A hawk darted from a neighboring evergreen, screaming as it flew.

The cave! The boys were close to it now. They dismounted, and noiselessly threaded their way among the underbrush, and up the uneven hillside. There were the two giant rocks which stood as sentries near the entrance.

The cave! All was silent without; no sound was heard from within. Slowly! slowly! noiselessly! The heavy stone door was reached.

*   *   *   *   *   *

When Louis Bowen felt the powerful grip of the sheriff, he made no effort to resist, but permitted himself to be bound hand and foot. Simpson, too, yielded without a struggle, and before they had time to realize what had happened, the two men were helpless prisoners.

The sheriff seized a heavy axe and began to destroy the still. The copper caldron was cut and battered beyond the possibility of repairs; the long pipes, usually called a worm, were twisted and broken; the iron of the furnace was shattered into fragments.

Old Bowen groaned and cursed alternately as he saw the work of years melt away before his eyes. Then he began to execrate the authors of his misfortune. The two boys, whom he had wished to kill had, no doubt, divulged the secret of the cave—why had he spared them? Why had he spared a Howard? The Howards had stood between him and his fortune for years; their upright, honest lives were a constant reproach to him; they had sheltered his runaway slave; Zachary Howard had spurned him, threatened to chastise him; Owen had saved the war message. If he could but take revenge! If he but had them in his power for a single hour! But even revenge was denied him, and he could but curse his enemies and bemoan his fate.

While the miserable wretch indulged in these fierce, but useless thoughts, Owen and Martin, the objects of his hatred, appeared in the dim, ruddy light at the door. With a frenzied cry of rage that rang through the rocky arches of the cave, and startled the sheriff, plying his work of destruction, Bowen snapped the rope that bound his hands, and jumped to his feet; but before he could disentangle himself and rush at the boys, Mr. Lane had seized him and laid him helpless on the floor.

"What brought you here?" the sheriff asked the boys, as he knelt with one knee upon the breast of his prisoner.

"We came to help you, Mr. Lane, for we feared you were in trouble," replied Owen.

"How did you find the way?"

"Find the way!" gasped old Bowen. "They were here—last fall—and promised—on their oath—to tell no one. If I had only killed them, I should not be a ruined man to-day," continued he, in half smothered tones.

"And we kept our word, Mr. Bowen," said Owen, in a faltering voice.

"Believe them, Mr. Bowen; they told no one," said the sheriff.

"Then—then—" stammered the captive, "Jerry and Stayford—have—have proved traitors! The whole—whole world is against me!"

"Boys," said Mr. Lane, "let's finish this here work as soon as we can. Pile them there barrels together to burn, and put shavings under that there wood; we'll set fire to 'em and leave this here place for good."

The boys began their work without answering a word. Scattered here and there were a number of large barrels in which the mash was prepared; these were rolled together in a heap. Along one side of the cave, and extending its entire length, was a pile of many cords of wood. Most of it was well seasoned poplar, with its thin, ragged bark hanging down on all sides. While Martin set fire to the barrels, Owen applied a brand to the dry bark. It burned like tissue paper; it hissed and sparkled, and sent up puffs of unsteady smoke which wrought strange shadows on the sides of the cave, and made the myriads of water-drops overhead tremble and glitter.

Soon the pile of wood began to burn, and as the fire grew brighter and brighter, it leaped to the top of the damp stone arches, tossed and flared and scattered showers of whirling sparks. The men and boys were dazzled by the sudden and brilliant flame. Huge columns of pitchy smoke rose up from the glowing mass. The heat became intense; so intense that Mr.

Lane cut the ropes which bound the prisoners and led them to the outer section of the cave; but he kept close to them, pistol in hand.

Two passages which led farther beneath the ground offered a natural flue through which the flame roared with the fury of a whirlwind. Stored away on heavy beams within these deep recesses of the cave were hundreds of barrels of whisky, the output of three years. The barrels caught fire; the heavy beams caught fire; the whisky poured out in streams and fed the raging element. Smoke and flame found their way through a thousand crevices and rifts until the whole hillside appeared to be ablaze. The glare through the rock door which stood ajar lit up the surrounding trees; while far below the glimmering river seemed a stream of blood.

The men and boys stood without, shading their faces from the heat and light, viewing the terrible and destructive scene. Old Bowen the while peered through the open door into one corner of the cave where a few pieces of wood lay half buried in the damp earth. The flames could not reach this wood, but the surrounding heat was gradually drying it. It began to smoke, then suddenly burst into a flame. At the same instant Louis Bowen shrieked: "Powder! powder!" he cried, as he sought in vain to free himself from Mr. Lane's grasp. "A barrel of it! The fire is over it! Run, run!"

He had scarcely uttered the last word when the whole hill seemed shaken to its foundation. A part of the stony vault fell with a crash, leaving a spacious chasm through which the pent-up flames burst with a mighty roar and leaped to the very top of the surrounding trees. A fragment of stone struck old Bowen and laid him lifeless at the feet of the sheriff. In the confusion which followed, Simpson darted into the woods and disappeared.

Mr. Lane and the boys fled from the spot to escape the suffocating smoke and flames. To their horror they saw the two giant rocks which had stood as guardian genii at the entrance of the cave start from their foundations and threaten to overwhelm them. For untold ages rain and frost and decay had done their work, and gradually removed the soil from beneath these stony masses, till it needed but the single shock of the explosion to set them in motion. At first they trembled with quick vibrations, then swung to and fro with the regularity of a pendulum, then rasped and jarred, and ground the stones beneath them into atoms, crushed the smaller trees which barred their progress, then on, on they dashed, gathering strength and terror as they went. Lane and the boys sprang aside just as they thundered by. Down, down they crashed; down, down, while the largest oaks and hickories bent as reeds before them, and were shivered into splinters—down, down, while the hills trembled beneath their massive weight and echoed with wild reverberations. At the water's edge they parted. One embedded itself in the mud and sand close to the shore; the other reached the middle of the river and disappeared beneath the water.

In the meanwhile the hill was shaken by another mighty throe—the entire roof of that section of the cave where the fire was raging collapsed and fell. The flame leaped out and lit up the trees and bluffs and river with a ruddy glow, and then was smothered and extinguished as if by magic. The sight was grand, but lasted only for a moment. A few gleams of light from the crevices in the hillside—a slight rumbling noise of the waves against the giant rocks—then all around was left in silence and in darkness.

CHAPTER XXVI.

Sealed Forever.

"THE WHOLE CAVE has fallen in," exclaimed Owen, as he leaped to the top of the cliff just in front of the place where the two giant rocks had stood.

"See, too, how the rocks are burned and blackened," replied Martin.

"I'm not surprised; I thought the whole world was on fire."

"And I thought that the Day of Judgment had come."

"Look at those trees! how they were crushed by the rocks."

"And the size of that rock!"

"It's as large as three houses."

"Now I see why the earth shook so much," said Martin. "I couldn't understand how one barrel of powder could make such an earthquake."

"And how do you explain it now?" inquired Owen of his companion.

"Easily enough; the whole cave was but a shell. The earth had been washed from around the rocks, and they were resting one on the other. When one fell, they all fell."

"What you say seems to be true," assented Owen.

"And now I wonder whether the whole cave has fallen in?" inquired Martin.

"Has Jerry's 'hold out' been blown up? That's the first question to answer," said Owen.

"Come," said Martin. "Let's see if we can find the little window."

It was the fourth day after the capture of old Bowen. Martin and Owen had come down to examine the scene of the explosion, and to search for the money which was supposed to be in Jerry's abode; for Mr. Lane had told them of the conversation which he had overheard between Simpson and the Tinker. In fact, the sheriff had promised to accompany them, but had been detained by business connected with his office. If they found the money, the two boys intended to send it on to the old trapper, who had always been friendly to them, and whose misfortune they both lamented.

It was impossible to judge of the position of the "hold out" from the top of the ridge where the boys were standing, so they descended into the ravine to the left of the hill to look for the small glass window.

With the exact description which Mr. Lane had given, they did not anticipate any great trouble, yet so ingeniously had Jerry concealed the opening, that they spent an hour without discovering it, although they passed below it many times.

Finally Martin suggested that one of them climb a tree near the cliff. He had scarcely finished the sentence before Owen, springing up to the lower branches of a young ash tree, mounted to the top as nimbly as a squirrel, and a moment later a shout of triumph announced to Martin that the window had been found.

"Can we get up to it?" asked Martin.

"It is best to get down to it," came the reply from the top of the tree. "How long are the ropes which we used to tie our horses?"

"They are over ten feet."

"Well, the longest will do. It's about seven feet from the window to the top of the cliff, whereas it is fully fifteen to the bottom, so you see it will be easier to climb down. I'll stay here while you go up on the ridge; then we'll be able to mark the exact spot over the window."

"That's a good scheme. It won't take me long to get up there," and Martin started off at once.

He gained the spot and called out for Owen. No answer came. He looked around to see whether he could have missed the place. No, it could not be; there was the ridge, there the ash tree which Owen had climbed. He waited for some time, then called again: "Owen! Owen!"

He heard the breaking of twigs behind him, and looking around beheld his friend, pale and trembling.

"Owen, what has happened?" he asked.

"I saw a ghost."

"What?"

"A ghost—a bear—something. I don't know what it was."

"Where?"

"In the window—just a moment—then it jumped back again."

"Why, Owen, you're dreaming. You fell asleep."

"No, I saw it. It was ugly, the ugliest thing I ever saw. Its face was covered with hair. It had large black eyes—I tell you, Martin, there was no dream about it."

"Sit down and cool off. Why, I never saw you so excited."

"Have your pistol ready, if it comes after us," said Owen, as he sat down on a log, and wiped the perspiration from his brow. "You had scarcely gone," he continued, "I was looking at the window, thinking of the night we spent in the cave, thinking of what we said about the ghosts when we were left alone in the dark. Then I saw the window slowly open and this ghost, thing, or bear, or whatever it was, looked at me with its two big eyes. You should have seen me get down that tree. I simply fell down; and away I went, looking back every minute to see whether the thing was following me."

"I never saw you frightened before. But I tell you what it is, Owen, I'm going to crawl into that window and see what's there."

Owen pleaded with Martin not to go; but the latter was firm in his resolution. As the boys talked Owen's curiosity grew stronger, until finally he consented to stand above the window and keep guard while Martin entered the cave. The rope brought, Martin knotted it in several places, leaving a loop at the end in which to rest his foot, then tied it to a small sapling just above the window.

Martin began his descent slowly, and not without some hesitation. When he reached the end of the rope he gave a scream which made the heart of his companion leap within him. Owen looked over the precipice, and, to his surprise and horror, saw a long, shaggy arm and rough claw slowly dragging Martin into the cave; yet he could not shoot for fear of hurting his companion. Martin the while struggled in vain. He felt the claws of an animal sink deep into his flesh; he felt himself being slowly drawn farther and farther into the window, and a sickly, dizzy feeling came over him. Everything around began to swim. He relaxed his hold on the rope. He heard the report of Owen's revolver. Then he was free, and was falling headlong down the side of the precipice. The thick grapevines protected him from the rocks, and somewhat broke the weight of his fall—for a moment, even entirely checking his perilous descent; and in that instant's pause he wildly clutched a strong branch, and then fell heavily to the ground.

The boy sprang to his feet, surprised to find that he had sustained no injury.

"Run, Owen! run!" he called out to Owen, who was standing at the edge of the cliff, pistol in hand.

Away the two boys went scudding through the woods like frightened rabbits.

"Are you hurt?"

"No."

"What was it?"

"A bear."

"That's what I told you. You wouldn't believe me."

"I believe you now."

"Was it a big one?"

"As big as an ox."

"Are you sure it didn't hurt you?"

"I thought it was eating my arm and leg off; but I don't feel it now."

"I thought you were a dead man when I saw you fall."

"The grapevines saved me."

The two boys all the while were saddling their horses and preparing for flight in case the animal followed them. They were suddenly startled by a noise in the opposite direction. It was Mr. Lane, who had finished his work and had come to join them in their sport.

"Halloo, youngsters! tired of the cave?" he asked. "Why, you look scared. What's the matter?"

"There's a bear in the cave," muttered Owen.

"Why, there isn't a bear in this here state, boy."

"Yes there is," stammered Martin. "He's as big as an ox. Both of us saw him."

Mr. Lane sat down and listened to the boys. Now that their giant friend was with them, Martin and Owen were no longer frightened. They succeeded in convincing Mr. Lane that there was really a bear or some other wild animal in the cave; although when Martin bared his leg where the monster had sunk his claws, he found only a light bruise.

The sheriff commanded the boys to follow him, determined that he would have its hide whatever the beast might be.

But how was he to get at the monster? Certainly he could not crawl through the small window, and neither Martin nor Owen would volunteer to go into the den and drive the animal out for him.

While they were consulting about the difficulty, Elijah, the runaway slave, suddenly appeared and began asking the pardon of the two boys for frightening them.

It will be remembered that Elijah had escaped from old Bowen some months previous, because the latter threatened to kill him. He was the only one of Bowen's slaves who knew of the existence of the cave, as he had assisted his master in hauling the still from Louisville and in putting it in position, and now that his master was dead, he had come to the cave to look for the money which he knew old Bowen had hid somewhere.

It was his intention simply to frighten the two boys. For this purpose he had used an old mask of deer skin, which Jerry had left behind him in the cave. But when he saw how scared the boys really were he repented of his act, for they had always befriended him.

A general laugh followed the explanation.

Elijah assured the boys that there was no money in the "hold out."

The four then went to review the scene, the negro acting as guide. He had worked for many days and nights in the cave, and was familiar with all its winding passages. In his opinion not more than a third of it had collapsed, but this in falling had entirely blocked the three entrances. Every hole and cranny on the roof of the cave and along the ridges was examined, but with no success.

"I reckon that old cave is shut up as tight as a fruit can," said the sheriff.

"Yes," replied Owen, "it is sealed forever."

"The 'hold out' isn't sealed," said Martin.

"I'm going to crawl into it and take a last look."

Both boys crept in through the little window. Martin put on the mask which Elijah had used, and looked out at Mr. Lane, who was standing below.

"Great pos-sim-mons," ejaculated the old marksman. "That looks just like the old Nick himself. 'Course you boys was scared when you seen such a crittar. I don't call you cowards no more. 'Course you run, and you was right."

While the sheriff amused the two with his remarks, Owen stood gazing at the huge rock which had fallen so as to bar completely the entrance to the cave from the "hold out."

"Martin," said he, in a broken voice, "I never in my life felt sadder or more disappointed than I do just now. We talked about this cave for days and weeks and months. I've thought of it; I've dreamt of it. I've looked forward to the time when we would wander through it with our torches, and tell the visitors of the first night we spent here. Now this is all impossible. The cave on the Beech Fork is sealed forever." On the floor he found a piece of charcoal. With it he wrote on the stone, which barred the way to the cave, the words:

Sealed Forever.

* * * * * *

On the old stage-road between Louisville and Nashville, near the banks of the Beech Fork, where stood the home of the Howards, can be seen to-day a spacious stone residence. In the attic of this house in the year 18—, a young boy of fifteen—a Howard— found a faded and dusty manuscript with the title, "The Cave by the Beech Fork," by Richard Lane. On the second page he read the following: "Richard Lane, generally called Coon-Hollow Jim, for years held the prize as the best marksman in the State. He was Sheriff of Nelson County for two successive terms, and ended his days as school-teacher in the Beech Fork district. He wrote an account of the famous shooting-matches of Kentucky, as also a history of the wonderful cave of Tom the Tinker. He has also left a description of a trip to New Orleans on the Woodruff."

The boy read the manuscript with intense interest. One scene described there was perfectly familiar to him. Often had he fished from Big Rock, and swam and rowed around Middle Rock. Could these be the huge monsters that thundered down the river bank and crushed the giant oaks on that eventful night? Even during the time of Mr. Lane they bore the names of Big Rock and Little Rock! How strange it all seemed. And the cave, could it be there? And the "hold out"?

He would see that very day whether it could be found. To the cave he went, the manuscript in hand, and with him John Finn, a companion, who shared with him his sports. What appeared to be the sunken roof of the cave was easily traced. In fact it was familiar to the boys as they had often hunted rabbits there in the thick hazel and sassafras bushes. The day passed by and the "holdout" was not found. The boys did not grow disheartened. They returned to the spot with a rope ladder; with this they could descend safely and examine the precipice by sections.

Their patience was at last rewarded. The "hold out" was found. Into it they climbed. The place was dry; the dust was inches deep upon the floor. Not a single object was seen. But there upon the rock could still be read the words:

Sealed Forever.

*   *   *   *   *   *

To-day a primitive ladder leads up into the "hold out." It is made of a sycamore trunk, nailed with slats and leaning against the side of the cliff. The "hold out" is a favorite resort for the boys during the fishing season, for here they seek protection from the Spring rains. This, too, is their place of lodging when they fish at night. Gathered here in dusky groups around a blazing camp-fire, they often sit and rehearse the story of Owen Howard and the cave by the Beech Fork.

Adventure Books for Boys
by Father Henry S. Spalding, S.J.

Stories that combine the Love of Country
with Love of the Catholic Faith

Cave by the Beech Fork
The Sheriff of the Beech Fork
The Race for Copper Island
The Marks of the Bear Claws
The Old Mill on the Withrose
The Sugar Camp and After
The Camp by Copper River
At the Foot of the Sand Hills
Held in the Everglades
Signals from the Bay Tree
In the Wilds of the Canyon
Stranded on Long Bar

"In *The Cave by the Beech Fork* a new genre is credited in American
Catholic Literature...all the fresh air books provided for boys had hitherto
been written by non-Catholics, and the lessons taught were the commercially
virtuous maxims of Benjamin Franklin, which are so devoid of spiritual life
as those of Polonius in his famous counsels to his son Laertes...A dozen
more books as true, as interesting, as honestly religious,
as manly as that, are, we hope, to be expected from his pen."

—Maurice Francis Egan (1852-1924), American Catholic Writer and Diplomat

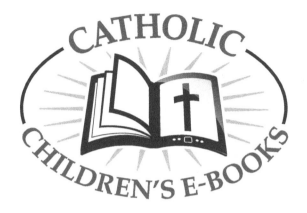

Our Catholic Heritage Digitized

- Exclusively Catholic
- Pre-K through College
- All e-Readers and Tablets Supported
- Books Added Monthly

www.CatholicChildrensEbooks.com

Printed in the USA
CPSIA information can be obtained
at www.ICGtesting.com
LVHW091204011123
762292LV00001B/41

9 781936 639465